THE LAST
WILD RIDE

THE LAST WILD RIDE

LEE MARTIN

ISBN: 1539477886
ISBN 13: 9781539477884
Library of Congress Control Number: 2016917224
CreateSpace Independent Publishing Platform
North Charleston, South Carolina

DEDICATION

To my lovely sister and best friend, Arlene, and in memory of our dear mother and brothers, Jack, Don, and Wesley.

Chapter 1

In the early spring of 1877 in northwestern Colorado, dangerous but gently rolling land lay marked with snow patches among scattered yellow-green stump junipers, waist high to a man, and lonely pinyon pine, dark green on red bluffs. A playground for black-tailed jackrabbits, prairie dogs, and the deadly red-tailed hawk, the land had a deceptively peaceful look.

In the far, distant east, snow and clouds blanketed the Rockies, while here in the ratty cow town of Red Hat on a miserable, overcast Saturday afternoon, nasty cold cut to the bone.

It made for ill tempers.

But Sam Jeffries, ill-tempered in every kind of weather, hardly knew the difference. At forty-one, he—a beat-up, shot-up, disgruntled, unshaven, raunchy former deputy US marshal—made no bones about his deep, burning resentment of the world around him.

Although handsome with broad shoulders, a strong jaw, and dark, flashing brown eyes, his attitude overshadowed his looks. His dark-brown hair hung collar length and unruly but was held in place by a black, wide-brimmed hat. A blue, double-breasted army shirt looked discolored under his leather vest.

In a dark, hand-tooled gun belt, Sam wore his army Colt tied down from his right hip. Sam, spoiling for a fight, swaggered into the Red Hat Saloon, his presence startling.

Men at tables turned their faces away and pulled their hats down.

Sam glared around the crowded saloon. It had no women. It smelled of smoke, rot-gut whiskey, nasty tobacco juice, dirty spittoons, and grimy sweat. The skinny barkeep with the long face kept busy behind the room-length walnut bar, where several men were standing with their backs to Sam.

A place for gambling and getting away from women folks, the saloon hosted cowhands and ranchers with only a few town citizens mingling. It had no wheels or other types of gambling fixtures—just tables and cards, cussing, and occasional laughter.

The men at the tables were not Sam's target.

Sam looked at the mirror behind the bar to see the faces of the men lined up in front of it. His mouth curved down on one side as he found his mark.

At the middle of the bar stood Hoag Ramsey, a handsome thirty-six-year-old, chunky, hard-faced rancher with pale-brown eyes, wearing a new brown hat and dark blue store- bought suit with fancy striped vest. With his boots spit polished, his gun belt tooled with his brand—the Rocking R—Hoag, though a dangerous man, looked as happy as if he had just found a glory hole.

At Hoag's right stood Corley, an aging, swarthy gunman with a smoke dangling from his surly mouth. Corley had sharp features, a crooked nose, and a thin, black mustache. He wore a silver-studded gun belt. A deadly shot, he only attached himself to winners like the wealthy Hoag.

Ramsey's men, their backs to Sam, crowded the bar on either side of Hoag and Corley.

Hoag, not seeing Sam off to the side, grinned at himself in the mirror behind the bar. He raised his glass like a man celebrating something grand.

"Drink up, men. I got me scalps on the tack room, a big new set of horns over my front door, and a share of the biggest cattle ranch in Colorado. But I tell you, one and all, it ain't nothing compared to what I got coming this very day."

Hoag downed his drink and pounded his chest once.

"I'm getting hitched to the prettiest woman west of the Mississippi."

Sam didn't like what he had just heard.

Sam made his move, snorted like a grizzly, and pushed between Hoag and Corley, shouldering them aside to make room for himself.

Hoag and Corley snarled and fell back along the bar—Hoag to Sam's left, Corley to Sam's right.

"What the hell?" Hoag growled.

"You smell something?" Corley asked Hoag. "I think some wild hog got in here."

Sam, ignoring them, ordered apple cider.

The skinny bartender, getting real nervous, served Sam and wandered away quickly.

Sam tasted the warm cider and smacked his lips, daring anyone to comment.

Sam leaned his left elbow on the bar, putting his back to Hoag.

Corley, now facing him, looked ready for a fight.

"That ain't a man's drink," Corley said.

Sam looked into his glass and took another long sip. He smacked his lips.

Hoag ground his teeth behind Sam.

"Look at 'im," Hoag snarled. "Lacey took his badge away on account of he went loco. Tearing up the town, shooting everything in sight. Yelling and kicking like a crazy man."

Corley downed his drink and laughed at Hoag's words.

Sam kept his back to them as he looked in the big mirror behind the bar and watched their faces. Having killed Hoag's brother sometime back, he knew Hoag had a need to shoot Sam full of holes.

"That bad, huh?" Corley grunted.

Hoag nodded. "Right after he killed his own wife."

Sam kept his mouth tight, curling it up on one side. Ready to explode, he stood and waited, narrowing his eyes.

"Yeah, and the fellah she run off with," Corley sneered, backing away.

Sam spun and slammed his fist into Hoag's face, knocking him back against the next man, who sent others falling or scattering.

Hoag nearly went down, grabbing the bar for support.

Sam backed away from the bar, kept backing to the center of the room and to the side.

Hoag's eyes blazed hot. His nose bleeding, he worked his mouth as a madman would. He wiped it with the back of his left hand. He winced at the pain but glowered at Sam.

Corley moved away from the bar, lower lip curled down, a hand near his holster. Men around them scrambled out of the lines of fire.

Hoag, nose still bleeding, backed up to a few feet from Corley. The crowd continued to scramble away from the fight. The bartender hurried to the far end of the bar and crouched down out of sight.

The three angry men stood alone in the center of the room. Hoag and Corley, side by side, glared at Sam.

"You're a poor loser," Corley mocked.

Hoag nodded and laughed at Sam but only for a second.

Death hovered around them. Hoag sobered with deadly intent.

The room fell dangerously silent.

Hoag's and Corley's right hands dangled next to their holsters.

The men around them moved even farther back, as far out of the line of the fire as they could. The skinny barkeep had disappeared.

Sam stood ten feet away, a hand near his holster.

Spectators held their breath.

Corley moistened his lips, readying for the kill.

Sam held his stance, waiting, watching.

Smoke hovered with the rank smell of the spittoons, the scent of whiskey, and the ever-present sweat.

"Look at 'im," Hoag snarled to Corley. "He's foaming at the mouth."

The crowd held back in a hush.

Sam's burning gaze moved slowly from Hoag to Corley and back again.

Hoag and Corley spread their feet. Blood curled down from Hoag's nose and into his mouth. He spat. Corley hunched, eagerly picturing Sam dead at his feet.

Hoag spat again. He reached for his Colt. Corley slapped leather.

Sam's Colt flew into his hand.

The deep breath of the crowd was heard.

Hoag, his weapon half out of his holster, stood frozen. Corley held his Colt partly out of his holster. For a long, frightful moment, the crowd could only stare.

Hoag and Corley both knew if they finished their draw, one or both of them would die. Sweat formed on their faces and necks. They could not move.

Sam's Colt, hammer drawn back, held them motionless.

"He can't get us both," Hoag growled.

Yet both Hoag and Corley hesitated, weapons still half in their holsters. Snickers from the crowd hit Hoag like a burning fuse.

Sam waited like a rattler.

The sudden entrance of a lawman froze the action.

US Marshal Lacey, middle-aged, stiff in movement, scars on his clean-shaven face, graying handlebar mustache, walked in through the swinging doors with a shotgun in hand. His badge on his tattered leather vest, his range clothes, and a battered, sweat-marked hat conveyed long days and nights spent on the trail. He looked weary and right impatient.

Everyone knew Lacey had no hesitation to kill.

And no one here wanted to die, except maybe Sam.

Hoag and Corley let their weapons slide back in their holsters.

Hoag wiped blood from his face and mouth with his trembling left hand. Hate blazed in his pale-brown eyes. His lips curled to keep back his angry words.

Lacey, shotgun ready, moved to the side of the action.

Corley spoke first, his voice searing. "There's a crazy man in here."

Lacey glared from one to the other, then at Hoag. "You start this?"

"Look, marshal, all I want is to get married. Soon's the stage comes in." Hoag paused to wipe his bloody nose with the back of his hand. "We was celebrating when Jeffries comes charging in like a wild bull."

Lacey moved into a better position with his shotgun.

Corley sneered. "Do something about him, Lacey, or we will."

Lacey turned to look at Sam, who slowly holstered his weapon. Lacey nodded toward the street and waved his shotgun, ordering Sam outside.

Sam walked ahead of Lacey, out the doors, onto the boardwalk, and away from the dirty windows. The saloon, just around the corner from the west side of the main street, had a dozen nervous saddle horses at the rails.

Lacey led Sam away from the saloon and around to the main street. Both felt the cold through their heavy coats and right through their britches. Their legs turned numb as they walked. Their boots felt heavy. Their hands and faces felt the threat of frostbite.

Both Sam and Lacey stopped to pull on their leather gloves.

They stood north of the hotel and town hall, which were both on the east side.

The small town seemed quiet enough. Riders. Wagons. Big business at the general store, its goods hanging around outside, under the eaves, for trade, the busy gunsmith with rifles at the window, and the not-so-busy express office.

Because of the severe cold, only men moved about. Mostly cowhands, ranchers, and business men in heavy clothes were on the boardwalks, but all were hurrying inside as soon as they could. A black dog trotted across the street and down an alley. All seemed peaceful but nearly frozen, even as the day, still overcast, began to warm.

Lacey walked with Sam up the street and then crossed over to the east side. They stopped at the rail in front of the express office, where Sam's buckskin gelding, tall with a black, flowing mane and tail, stood tied. Sam had a bedroll, possible sack, canteen, and lariat on his saddle.

Lacey, clearly irritated as he balanced his shotgun, finally found his voice, which cast steam in the air. "Sam, I told you to get out of town."

"I'm in no hurry."

"You're bound and determined to get yourself killed."

"I was minding my own business."

"Yeah, in Ramsey's saloon, knowing they hate your guts."

Sam moved off the boardwalk as Lacey waited. Sam stroked the nose of his buckskin as it nudged him. It concentrated on Sam's vest. Sam dodged around the not-so-friendly nibble.

"Or are you forgetting you killed Ike's brother?" Lacey persisted.

Sam shrugged, never able to forget killing any man in a fight.

Lacey put his hand on the railing. He looked around as if expecting Hoag and Corley to reappear. The sun tried to escape the dark cloud.

Lacey continued. "Sure, you were wearing a badge and it was a fair fight, but Ike's had you in his sights ever since."

"I don't need a badge for killing snakes."

"Sam, settle down and face the facts. Ramsey owns this half of Colorado. He has his own army. If I were you, I'd head for Tennessee. See your folks."

Sam removed his hat, ran his hand over his damp hair. "They're on the Mississippi. On a river boat to New Orleans, then over to Fort Worth."

"Second honeymoon?"

"They're still on the first."

Sam paused to glance at Lacey, who had been grieving for ten years over the loss of his own wife and child to cholera. Lacey would never enjoy a second honeymoon, nor would he see his son become a man.

Sam, watching Lacey's sad face, quickly changed the subject. "Besides, I filed on some land near Elk Creek."

"That's only a whoop and a holler south of here."

"Gonna raise horses," Sam said.

Lacey adjusted his hat, pulled it on again, and shook his head. "You shamed Hoag back there. And you probably broke his nose."

"He asked for it."

"Yeah, I bet." Lacey gestured. "If you get down to Elk Creek, I don't figure Sheriff Tyree's going to hold your hand. Didn't he throw you in jail for breaking up the saloon?"

"Yeah, and we went fishing the next day." Sam grinned. "He's coming in with me, soon's he retires."

"I'm real sorry for him. You got a stick of ornery up your..." Lacey paused, nodded up the street. "Stage is early."

Sam looked over the saddle as he and Lacey, still on the boardwalk, watched the weather-beaten stage with four weary bays as it came from the north, rumbled past them, and pulled up with a bounce in front of the faded, two-story hotel down the street on the same side and farther south.

They watched in silence as Potts, a bearded, aging driver with disheveled clothes, climbed down, spat tobacco juice, and moved toward the side near the boardwalk to drop the steps. Potts, crippled by old age, never stopped living his life as he chose.

Potts helped a well-dressed, gorgeous, thirty-year-old woman down from the stage.

At that very moment of her appearance, bright sunlight burst through the clouds as if to announce her arrival. She bathed in the glow, which seemed to center on her very presence.

Sam and Lacey could only stare.

She wore a heavy, blue cape with the hood fallen back from her long, golden hair. Despite being weary and cold, she radiated warmth and goodness as she smiled at Potts.

Sam and Lacey stared in disbelief as the sunlight continued to shine on her.

Sam felt a twinge of longing, something that pain had suppressed long ago in his gut. She probably could make any man give up the whole world to be with her, but to Sam, she was a woman—which meant trouble.

"Lorena Meredith," Lacey said, "from Kansas. Here to marry up with Hoag Ramsey."

Now they had a better look at her face. Gazing at her striking beauty, Sam and Lacey remained stunned. Her features were perfect. Her bright-blue eyes gleamed like a sunlit sky. She moved with grace unseen on the frontier.

Asa, her blond, ruddy-faced ten-year-old son, wearing a heavy coat but haphazardly dressed as if he had stripped off anything he disliked, hopped down to her side. Asa had darker-blue eyes and looked, for all the world, as if he didn't want to be here.

Sam and Lacey stood watching with awe from a distance.

Lacey adjusted his hat as he spoke. "Boy's name is Asa. He's mute. And she's a widow."

Sam stood wrapped in his own misery as he watched her and the boy.

"Hoag's done a lot of bragging." Lacey shook his head. "Knowing him, he only took the boy so he could have her."

Sam's anger burned at the very thought of Hoag putting his hands on this gorgeous woman. Yet Sam's bitter past experiences with women would not let him bend enough to grant this or any woman one bit of leeway. As far as he was concerned, not one of them could be trusted. He just didn't want Hoag Ramsey to be so lucky.

They watched as Lorena moved from the stage to the boardwalk in front of the hotel.

Lacey tugged at his hat brim. His voice grew deeper. "Hoag, he says the boy wasn't born mute, so he's going to make him talk."

Both Sam and Lacey reacted to the thought with a grimace.

Town folk stopped on both sides of the street to look at the arrivals.

No one paid attention to the other passengers, not even Silas Parker, a slick gambler with a heavy coat opened to show a fancy red vest, nor the elderly couple.

All eyes were on Lorena as she moved to the hotel entrance.

Asa stayed with the driver, who opened the boot.

Coming up the street, Luke, a young, freckle-faced cowboy on a bay horse, rode over by the stage and up to the boardwalk as he called to her.

"Mrs. Meredith?"

Lorena now turned as the rider gave her a message, which Sam and Lacey could just barely hear.

"Mr. Ramsey had trouble to take care of on the ranch," the young rider said.

"Thank you, mister…"

"Just Luke, ma'am. Mr. Ramsey, he allowed as how he'd be here for supper."

The cowboy turned his horse and rode back down the street.

Lorena paused, thoughtful. Parker, the gambler, quickly arrived at her side, looking ready to escort her, but she waved him to go inside as she turned to wait for her son. She stood in the sunlight that danced like gold in her flaxen hair.

Lacey and Sam had a hard time taking their eyes from her.

Lacey grinned. "Hoag's trouble at the ranch was stopping that nose bleed you gave him."

Sam mounted his buckskin gelding. He looked real ornery.

"Woman like that got no business with Hoag Ramsey," Lacey said. "I ought to arrest him."

"I should've killed him."

"And have Emma after you?" Lacey said with a chuckle. "I'd rather take on every one of her sons and their old man than face up to her."

Sam grunted and took up the reins.

"Hoag's her favorite," Lacey added. "She can't be happy about this."

Sam tried not to look at Lorena, but she had the look of a goddess—too good for the likes of any Ramsey. Staring at her, he could see her in a framed portrait over a mantle.

Lacey followed Sam's gaze. "You know, Sam, what your problem is? You don't really hate anyone but yourself."

Sam pulled his hat down tight, nodded to Lacey, and reined his horse, preparing to ride toward the south end of town. He would have to pass the coach.

Lacey turned away and headed in the other direction.

Lorena stood in front of the hotel. She turned to smile back down at her son. She looked amazing but seemed unaware of it. She had faced a frightening change and a lot of worry. After losing her husband in a wagon accident several years back, she bravely moved here to make a new life for her son.

Asa smiled up at her, then turned as Potts, the driver, removed some of the luggage from the boot. Asa pointed out which was theirs. The four bay horses in harness snorted, their heads down, and were still run with hot sweat that steamed in the cold.

Potts straightened up, stretched, wiped his mouth, and turned to Asa.

"Son," Potts said, "if I was your new pa, I'd have been waiting right here from sunup."

Asa, who never spoke, only shrugged.

As Sam rode south, closer to the coach on his left, he looked across at Lorena.

It pained Sam that Hoag's hands would be on her, and the sooner she left his sight, the better. Just the same, he tried to convince himself she had her eye on Hoag's fortune. He figured all women were all alike: once they set their hooks in you, you didn't have a chance.

Lorena saw him and seemed taken aback by his fearsome presence.

Sam, sour, tipped his hat. She gave a slight bow of her head.

Potts waved briefly at Sam, who nodded to him.

Asa came around the coach, causing Sam to rein up. Sam, an awesome figure, looked down at Asa. The boy stared up at him. Asa had never seen anyone so much bigger than life, as this fearsome rider was. The whole Wild West rode that buckskin.

For a long moment, Sam's fierce appearance remained just that, until Asa suddenly smiled at him. Sam, disarmed, briefly smiled back. For a long moment, they just looked at each other as if they were old friends.

Sam reached in his vest pocket, took out a small, folded knife about two inches long. He tossed it to the surprised boy, who caught it.

Lorena stood watching from the hotel entrance, but Sam rode on without another look at her. Her gaze followed him as he rode south toward the edge of town. She remained silent as if leery of Sam's wild demeanor and his departure.

Neither she nor Asa had ever seen such a man. They had both been taught that all men had good in them and never to hate anyone for his or her failings. But she had second thoughts as his image blazed in her memory. Sam almost, but not quite, blurred the loss of her first husband, Asa's father, a big and rugged man like Sam.

Sam appeared frightening yet so awesome; he was like their first glance at the Rocky Mountains—unbelievable.

At that moment, Silas Parker, the slick gambler, came back out of the hotel without his heavy coat. He looked the part with his fancy red vest, diamond stickpin, classy dark suit of clothes, a gold watch on a chain, and shiny black boots. He had greased black hair, a thin mustache and dark, gleaming eyes, but he wore a congenial smile.

A handsome man of forty, he had charm but could not inspire confidence in others. People around him often checked their pockets when he walked away.

As he joined Lorena, the sun retreated behind the clouds. The day grew darker.

Parker removed his hat. Kindness oozed from his smile. His Virginia accent had been tempered over the years. He had never put himself out for anything, not even the War Between the States, except for running contraband to the highest bidder.

Parker's real love was gambling, but he was open to offers, especially from a woman as beautiful as this. She could be the first one to keep his interest longer than a night.

He had left his heavy coat inside so that she could see what a dandy he was.

"Mrs. Meredith, can I be of service?"

"Thank you, Mr. Parker."

Parker took her arm, escorted her into the hotel.

Asa looked up to watch them go inside. He made a face. He didn't trust Parker or anyone else.

Asa walked into the street to look at Sam as he reached the far end of town, where the road would turn south. He had never seen such a man who could leave such a silent explosion behind him.

To his surprise, Sam reined up, turning his horse to look back. Sam lifted his hand to wave at Asa. The boy, startled, quickly waved at Sam.

Asa, delighted as he watched Sam fall out of sight, decided he would have trusted Sam and felt sorry to see him ride away. Asa fondled the knife before putting it in his pants pocket.

Potts put the luggage on the steps, then turned as Asa came back to his side.

"That was Sam," Potts said.

Asa silently turned to look at the driver, who continued to talk.

"I knew him in the War Between the States when we was still in uniform fighting Indians. After that, he was a lawman, but he lost his badge. He's been real mean of late."

Asa looked at him expectantly.

"Sam Jeffries," Potts added.

Asa grinned at the name. His grin kept growing wider until it hurt.

Potts chuckled. "Your ma know you read dime novels?"

Asa shook his head, could not stop grinning. Asa looked happy as they walked to the boardwalk. Potts had to chuckle again.

Inside the hotel, Parker and Lorena spoke while Asa went upstairs with a bellboy and the luggage. The clean, shiny lobby—vacant except for the old, balding man at the desk—was quiet. Toward the back, an entrance led to the fine-dining room, which looked empty.

Parker, infatuated with Lorena, couldn't help himself. Her golden hair and her bright-blue eyes were driving him.

"Maybe we could have supper," Parker suggested.

"I'm sorry. Mr. Ramsey will be here."

"I would have ridden out to meet you."

"But you don't have a ranch to run."

"I heard the Ramseys are big around here. Loaded with money."

She frowned, not liking the innuendo. "My son needs a father."

She gave him a look that put him in his place.

"I have news for you," Parker said. "Hoag Ramsey's going to send your boy off to boarding school, first chance he gets."

"You're wrong," she said icily. "Good evening, Mr. Parker."

Parker bowed, backed away, and watched her go up the stairs. Hunger in his dark gaze, he could not hide what he was thinking. He wanted that woman and determined to have her—sooner or later. He moistened his lips. A patient man, he could wait.

Potts, the driver, came to stand beside Parker.

"You're not very bright," Potts said. "You hang around her long enough, Hoag Ramsey will come after you and nail you to his barn door."

Potts looked around, then walked to a quiet, lonely space in the lobby. Parker stuck to his heels. Potts took a deep breath, looking around again.

Potts spoke softly. "Hoag's a killer."

"Just like that?"

"Nothing's ever been proven, but if you're smart, you won't be shooting off your mouth around any of them Ramseys. You won't see it coming." Potts looked around again. "The worst is Emma. You rub her the wrong way—that's it."

Parker, not impressed, turned to look up the staircase.

"Still, it would be worth it."

Potts watched him a moment, shook his head, and went back outside.

⚏

That evening in the hotel's dining room, Hoag sat with Lorena and Asa. She looked so beautiful in a dress that matched her blue eyes; Hoag could hardly stand his own joy.

The dining room boasted white tablecloths, burgundy drapes and rug, and a grand chandelier with kerosene lamps in glass holders. Candles burned in matching glass bowls along the walls. Four well-dressed couples sat at other tables.

Hoag, in a dark suit, looked big and handsome—despite the powdered-over bruise on his strong nose. He had just turned thirty-six. He was his mother's first-born and decided favorite, and he later took advantage of it at the ranch, lording the favoritism over his younger brothers and being surly with his cantankerous father.

His mother Emma opposed this marriage. She had dominated his life until that day in Kansas when Hoag had met this gorgeous woman, and now Emma would have to let go…or not.

The waiter, about sixty and bald, dressed in black with a white shirt and bow tie, acted stiff and pompous. His nose seemed stuck in an up position. He set glasses of water on the table and left to secure their orders.

Asa, neatly dressed and quiet, sometimes stared down. Other times, he watched Hoag as if waiting for something bad to happen. Hoag smiled at him. Asa didn't smile back until Lorena nudged him.

Asa had learned to be suspicious of every man who came near his mother. Hoag had made him nervous from first sight. And yet, having seen Sam Jeffries in the flesh, and despite the dime novels, Asa would have taken Sam's hand and walked anywhere with him. Asa liked that feeling with Sam. He didn't like his mother being anywhere near Hoag Ramsey.

Lorena, ever beautiful in her blue silk dress with black lace at the throat and wrists, sat quiet and ladylike. Her golden hair gleamed in the lamplight. When she looked at Hoag, his image did not blur the face of her late husband, not the way Sam had.

Lorena, subdued, questioned her wisdom, until she glanced at her son. He needed a father, and Hoag could give him everything. Hoag had promised to make a cowhand out of the boy. He had even convinced her that once Asa had a father again, the boy would start talking.

But Hoag didn't have Asa on his mind, not for a second. The boy meant nothing to him, except to corral this incredible woman. His gaze devoured Lorena and her unusual beauty, everything any man could ever want. He moistened his lips.

"The wedding's at noon tomorrow. My mother got it all set up," Hoag said. "You will like her."

Lorena smiled. "I'm sure I will."

"You too, Asa," Hoag said to the silent boy. "And my pa, Ike—he's a real fire eater, but he's the best there is. And there's my little brother Jonas; now he's shy around women. Harley, he's just the opposite, but he knows better than to get in my way."

Lorena tried not to look as nervous and remorseful as she really was. Oh, yes, Hoag had been a real gentleman when romancing her in Kansas with a lot of promises, and any young woman would be thrilled at his attention. Yet the long stagecoach ride had made her a little too thoughtful. Now she'd have less time to think about it. She'd be rushing into a new life for her and Asa.

She had explained to Hoag about her son. He knew why Asa had stopped talking at the age of five and why now, five years later, he was still silent. No doctor could change what had happened. Yet Hoag had promised once they were married, Asa would open up.

Except the boy meant nothing to Hoag as he watched her.

"Just wait until you see the ranch," Hoag said. "It's all fixed up for us. We'll have it to ourselves for a whole week. Ma will be at a neighbor's. Pa and my brothers will be driving cattle off to a buyer up north."

Lorena tried to look happy about it. When they had finished supper, Hoag did not smoke. Instead, he kept a clean image for her benefit.

"Asa needs his rest," she said at length.

Hoag got to his feet, hustled around to bring her chair back. Lorena stood, as did Asa.

Hoag escorted them to the foot of the stairs. He acted like he wanted to kiss her, but she held out her hand. He took her hand, bowed slightly, and let them go up the stairs. He would have his way soon enough.

When Lorena and her son were out of sight on the landing, Hoag grimaced and hurried outside. Night had fallen. Near the hotel, Corley waited in the shadows. Hoag left the hotel to join him in the pale light of the moon.

"Well?" Hoag demanded.

"Boys can't find him."

"How far could he get, for crying out loud?"

"Just plumb went and disappeared," Corley said.

"What about Lacey?"

"He says he don't know nothing."

"I want Jeffries dead," Hoag said, grimacing. "He shamed me. No man gets away with that."

"I was there, remember?" Corley looked through the hotel window at the staircase. "Right now, you've got other business." He grinned. "You're a lucky man."

"Except for the kid."

"You'll think of something."

"You can bet I will."

Chapter 2

The same night of Lorena's arrival in Red Hat, Sam Jeffries camped on a southern trail off in a rocky canyon cut into the bluffs. Above, dark pinyon pines stood as heavy sentinels against the starry sky. Stunted junipers with yellow-green leaves hugged the walls. Even wrapped in blankets, he shivered from his wide-brimmed hat to his cracked boots.

His fire burned hot, deep in a rock pit against the wall overhang that protected his camp. Its flickering light caught the glimmer of a spring that trickled down the rocks near him and his blanketed buckskin gelding.

Farther back but catching the light, serviceberry bushes hung heavy with clustered, drooping, white flowers. A chokecherry bush hovered nearby from the rustle of some critter unseen within it.

The sweet whistle of a chickadee somewhere in the bushes sounded once.

Sam finished his supper and leaned against the wall with his cup of coffee. He felt the cold icing his bones and frosting his face. Off in the night, the sudden bark of a lone coyote echoed into silence.

Sam heard a noise. He looked up through the clumped top of a twisted juniper and saw a nervous, gray porcupine slip to the ground and disappear in the dark.

Sam loved this country, especially the blazing sun that often gave way to storms with snow or hail. Nights would be cold, as they were now, leaving him stiff and weary, but a man could be alone here with his deepest thoughts.

Sam settled back and stared at the flickering fire.

Lacey's words echoed in his thoughts. *You just hate yourself.*

Sam grimaced. The truth was often too painful. He had expected to have the happy life his father and mother enjoyed. Even as a boy, he could see in them what he wanted for himself, but he had failed.

Sam had loved only one woman in his life. She had taken a rough frontiersman and tried to change him. He had bent as much as he could and had made it his mission to provide her with all the luxury she desired.

She had fought the idea of children, saying it was too dangerous and would ruin her figure. Her denial had broken his heart. Sam had let himself be manipulated and governed, leading to his becoming miserable. He hated himself for allowing that to happen.

In her final days, she had taught him one thing that would stay with him forever. Never again would he let a woman run his life. And never again would he let himself fall in love.

It had been a stab in his heart when he had seen Asa on the street. It had reminded him of the son he had been denied.

And despite himself, he remembered a montage of painful reflections: he saw *his wedding day*—the lovely Myra, her light-yellow hair in curls, wearing stark-white lace, standing at his side in the church. She had lovely brown eyes, heart-shaped lips, and a smile that made up his world.

"I love you, Sam," she had whispered.

He saw himself in *his officers uniform*—straight as an arrow, his heart full. But there she would be, glaring at him when he returned from a campaign, still alive and still all army. He could see her turn away as she demanded a better life.

Her voice echoed out of the past. "Sam, this is not the way I want to live."

And then saw *a badge on his chest*—his civilian clothes, his six-gun still smoking as he turned to see her in satin and velvet (clothes he couldn't afford), more jewelry that cast him further into debt, a look of scorn on her face.

"Everything's for you," she had said. "Nothing's for me."

He was suddenly *standing in their little house*—his badge gleaming from the lamplight as he tossed his bedroll on the table, glad to be home from a long ride, only to find her gone. Shaken, he read her note over and over, then picked up a chair and slammed it through the window, shattering the glass.

Memories so painful, he cut them short and shut them away.

Back in the present, he proceeded to lecture himself.

Here at his campfire in the night, he tried to bring himself to face the life he was leading—a life filled with anger and vengeance that would never be satisfied. Again, he fought to close off the past and to think only of this night.

He took out his pistol and emptied the shells. He started cleaning it but kept his loaded rifle handy. Once more, a coyote howled from far away. A lonely coyote.

⚔

On Sunday morning in Red Hat, the weather cleared, shifting into a cold but sunny day. The little community church perched on a sandy, red knoll. A small crowd partly filled the pews. The well-dressed merchants among them coveted the Ramseys' business but were afraid to cross them. Two of the merchants had brought their young, hopeful daughters, who were in their late teens and looking at the Ramseys' wealth.

Town leaders had been invited to the wedding and the whole town to the reception—everyone except Sam Jeffries and US Marshal Lacey, who both had already headed south on separate trails. Parker was nowhere to be seen..

In the whistle-clean church, the crowd included cleaned-up cowhands from the Ramseys' Rocking R and some hard cases with gun belts hidden under their Sunday-go-meeting coats. Others were either old timers who'd rather be fishing or young, fresh-faced hands trying to keep their jobs.

In the front pews sat Hoag's brothers and his parents.

In the front row of the left pew, Hoag's brother Jonas, twenty-four, had the same dark-brown hair but darker-brown eyes. While his brothers were chunky, Jonas had the broad shoulders and was more tan and leaner looking with his narrower hips. Jonas squirmed on the hard pew seat whenever one looked him over, including Nancy Madison, the lone survivor of a raid on her family's homestead, who was living in town with a widowed lady.

Jonas knew too much about his own family. He had watched how his father and brothers could put on the charm to fool the world, even though they had killed and murdered without hesitation. Even his mother's sweet charm hid the strength and determination of a woman whose men could do no wrong.

Yes, Jonas thought, they all had two faces, and he felt no pride.

Next to Jonas sat their father, Ike Ramsey, a graying, mustached hunk of a man who looked uncomfortable in his gray suit. A white scar striped his left cheek. At fifty-eight, he had a history that played across his face in every passing moment. He had no patience for any man. He had buried so many that he had lost count.

Stiff at his side, Emma tried to force a smile for the crowd. A handsome fifty-seven-year-old woman with tight skin and cold, pale-brown eyes, she had her graying hair up in waves that ended in a bun. She wore a dark-green dress with little frills. She looked uneasy sitting there in the church. She had only contempt for townspeople and expected every one of them to do her bidding. She resented Lorena's refusal to bend.

In fact, she had hated Lorena from first sight.

The gorgeous bride not only made Emma feel dowdy but also was stealing her favorite son, Hoag. Emma had always favored Hoag, her first-born, had always fussed over him, and had always taken his side in arguments, even against her husband. Oh, she loved and honored Ike—as long as he never laid a hand on Hoag.

The frontier life had hardened her beyond her natural grit. After Harley, she had lost two sons in childbirth and, later on, a little girl to fever. Three months after she lost her daughter, she journeyed to Cheyenne to see her dying mother. All the while, her own family had treated her like dirt, even though the Ramsey Ranch prospered while they struggled.

She had stood up to them and nature and the early days on the frontier.

Yet nothing had prepared her for losing her first-born to some strange woman with a young son who couldn't speak. But then, she would not have liked any woman to be with Hoag.

As the bride and groom stood in front of the skinny, squeaky-voiced preacher, listening to his spiel on the blessings of marriage, Asa, uncomfortable in a dark suit of clothes, stood aside looking miserable.

Hoag, finely dressed in a blue suit, his dark hair slicked down, had powdered his bruised nose again. His hurry to make Lorena his bride had cultivated a long-restrained hankering to get her in his clutches, which he bore through the months of his acting as a gentleman.

Lorena, unbelievably beautiful in a silver-blue dress with white lace at her wrists and throat, wore a white-lace mantilla draped over her long, golden hair. Her glistening, crystal-blue eyes and her sweet smile only hinted at the deep sadness in her heart.

She had one attendant, the preacher's dowdy wife, and had never felt so alone.

Hoag's brother Harley Ramsey, a thirty-two-year-old womanizer, gambler, and loose cannon, stood as the best man. He resembled Hoag in chunkiness and wore a similar dark-blue suit but appeared more seasoned and also more competitive. Harley hated how their mother had always favored Hoag. Whenever Hoag had done something great, Harley would try to take his glory away from him.

As Harley stood gazing at Lorena, he knew he would be a better man for her. He didn't drink as much as Hoag. He knew how to treat a woman. Hoag, heavy handed, could be mean.

With Harley's gaze fixed on her, Lorena felt all the more nervous.

Hoag held her hand as the preacher continued.

At last, the ceremony ended. On her ring finger, she wore a plain gold band. Hoag turned to pull Lorena close and planted his hungry kiss on her lips. Lorena felt a shiver run through her.

Asa and Harley followed them from the altar, and everyone turned and followed.

On the porch steps of the church, Hoag hurried Lorena, knowing his brothers would seek kisses from the bride. He took her hand and rushed her down to the walk, leading her toward the church hall, a nearby and simple building, for the reception.

❊

While Lorena and Hoag were being married in Red Hat, Sam Jeffries was making the long ride south toward Elk Creek, under clear skies. The trail grew rough on the red, sandy soil with silver on the sage. Pines lined the hills. To the far east rose the ever-beautiful Rockies, covered in snow and hovering clouds.

At times, he heard only his saddle.

The pungent scent of scattered sage could not mask the smell of his buckskin's sweat.

A black-tailed jackrabbit bounded from nearby brush, almost flying until it was out of sight. Sam always envied its freedom and wanderings. He welcomed the sight of black-tailed prairie dogs as they poked from the ground with their curious barks. He didn't even mind the occasional rattlers if they kept their distance.

Sam felt at home on the prairie.

He could see Elk Creek on the grassland just ahead.

A small cattle town, it had a reputation for being the tamest place in the new state of Colorado, but only because of Sheriff Tyree. It boasted one saloon, a livery, and a host of stores to serve the surrounding ranches. Boardwalks were cracked but often swept clean by the wind.

In the cold twilight, Sam rode into town on the same Sunday evening Lorena's wedding reception was occurring back in Red Hat. Yes, he hated women, but the breathtaking Lorena in the hands of Hoag Ramsey continued to be a real irritation.

Sam reined up in front of the sheriff's office. He dismounted in the fading light, left his buckskin at the railing, and saw no one on the street.

Sam walked into the toasty, warm sheriff's office like a charging grizzly. He stormed over to the hot iron stove, grabbed a coffee cup, and poured himself some of the thick, ugly black coffee. The hot liquid warmed his insides, but his hands and feet were still numb.

Sheriff Tyree didn't budge from his desk. He leaned back in his chair and wiped his face with his bandanna. He still wore his hat, and a star dangled on his leather vest. His trim, gray handlebar mustache graced a weary, expressive face. Crinkles surrounded his brown eyes and mouth. Tyree, now in his fifties, had experienced most everything in life, including war, yet he had not figured out how to deal with Sam.

"They get a new sheriff in Red Hat?" Tyree asked.

Sam paced around, looking mean. "No, but Lacey was there."

"He straighten you out?"

"Not a chance."

Tyree leaned forward, watching Sam stare out the window.

"Lacey passed through here this morning," Tyree said. "Mentioned Hoag Ramsey was getting married today."

"Yeah."

Tyree stood. "I never thought Emma would go for that."

"She won't."

"So the woman's from Kansas."

"Yeah."

"Got a son won't talk."

Sam nodded. "Nice kid."

"Lacey says she's a real looker." Tyree stood, came around his desk, and sat on the edge. "Is that what's bothering you? Hoag getting his hands on her?"

Sam grunted, having no answer, but Tyree had him pegged right.

"Sit down, Sam."

Sam turned, grunted, paced, and went back to the window.

"You know," Tyree said, "when I was in my twenties, I fell hook, line, and sinker for a farmer's daughter. Her pa run me off, and that was the end of it, but I ain't looked at another woman since. So here I am—an old bachelor and sorry for it."

Sam continued to stare out the window, not bothering to answer.

"Don't make that mistake," Tyree said. "Being alone ain't natural."

⧈

Back in Red Hat that same evening, there were two-dozen townspeople inside the church hall, well-dressed men and women lingering after the wedding. Two young, single, very pretty women paraded their ambition to marry a Ramsey.

Everyone did business with the Ramseys, but no one liked them—until Lorena and Asa came to town. She and her son were happily received and admired on sight, but the wedding left her short of breath.

Decorations readied the hall for merriment. Food and drinks lined tables. A fiddler stood up, ready to play.

Asa reached the table of cookies and tarts. A merchant's kindly wife greeted him and began feeding him with everything in sight.

The crowd milled, waiting for the wedding couple. The necessity of catering to the Ramseys stuck in the craw of many, but no one complained while armed men watched over the proceedings.

Now the bride and groom made their way inside.

Harley caught up with the new couple.

"Stand aside, Brother," Harley said. "Let a real man kiss the bride."

Emma stepped in front of the passionate Harley and glared up at him.

"You will treat Hoag's bride with respect," Emma said with her icy voice, which so easily controlled her men. "On the cheek. Gently."

Lorena wasn't sure whether Emma meant to protect her or Hoag or whether Emma just didn't want her boys kissing a strange woman.

Emma let Harley give Lorena a kiss on the cheek. Lorena shivered under Harley's wet lips. Hoag drew her free of Harley.

Emma let the shy Jonas shake Lorena's hand.

Emma gave Ike the devil's eye. Ike got the message. He kissed Lorena on the cheek.

Hoag pulled her back out of reach as the fiddler played a waltz. Hoag took Lorena to the floor, danced grandly with her. All eyes followed this really beautiful bride.

Then others joined in, with Harley claiming the prettiest of the young women who had marriage on their minds. Another young lady dragged the bashful Jonas onto the floor, but he excused himself as soon as the music stopped.

Jonas turned to see Nancy Madison, barely nineteen, standing among the townspeople. Nancy, also shy but pretty in gingham, had large blue eyes, dark-brown hair in ringlets, and a turned-up nose. She never knew who had murdered her family four years ago while she was away at school. She had always suspected the Ramseys, and she believed Jonas might have the answers. She walked over to him.

Jonas did have the answer, which made him squirm.

"Jonas, please dance with me," she said, offering her hand.

Jonas looked from her to his angry, glaring mother. Nancy took his hand, and he drew her into his arms, swaying with her on the dance floor among the crowd.

"Are you afraid of me, Jonas?" Nancy asked in a low voice.

He nodded, and she smiled, moving closer. They both knew Emma wanted Jonas to have nothing to do with her.

Emma's need to protect her husband and sons from the law drove her to intensely dislike Nancy, fearing that Jonas would say something to Nancy that would put them at risk.

Emma signaled to Harley, who left his women to cut in on Jonas and whirl Nancy away from him. Nancy acted polite to Harley but did not like him.

Watching but not mixing, the Ramsey gun hands knew better than to rile Emma.

Two of them, Crowe and Crenshaw, both in their forties, similar in attitude and dress, kept their gun belts hidden under their Sunday coats, but each had his own brutal history.

Crowe, a man with beady eyes and thin beard, had been an outlaw most of his life. He had always taken what he wanted—whatever the cost.

Crenshaw, raunchy with his fancy boots, looked like a dandy, but could be just as deadly. He fancied himself as being better than anyone else with his draw or with women.

⧗

The Ramsey ranch, north of Red Hat, stretched wide with rolling hills. Junipers dotted the landscape, and grass grew strangely plentiful and jealously guarded. Cattle and horses grazed in the far distance. Clouds in the east spread over the snow-crested Rockies. Here, the setting sun promised it would be another freezing night.

The barn and sheds appeared all in good order. Horses in the corral looked sassy and well fed. The big, two-story house and picket fence gleamed with recent whitewash. Flowers struggled to survive in the garden's red, gravely soil.

At twilight, the newlyweds had the big house to themselves, except for Asa, who had gone to bed early in his room on the first floor.

The house boasted rich rosewood furnishings, expensive art, lush carpeting, and blue-velvet drapes. A piano gleamed from polish. Paintings of the west and antique weapons graced the walls.

No ranch gear could be brought inside, but weapons were everywhere.

Downstairs by the hearth, standing alone with a glass of whiskey in his hand, Hoag worked himself up, fighting for courage to approach this incredible woman he had managed to rope and tie. He downed his drink, poured himself another, and downed it too.

Hoag gathered himself up and headed for the master bedroom at the top of the stairs.

One step at a time, Hoag convinced himself this would be a happy occasion. He reached the door to the master bedroom, walked in, and stopped in dismay.

Lorena turned from the mirror to smile at him. She wore a blue-silk negligee and nightgown the color of her eyes. Her golden hair cascaded down her shoulders. She tried not to be afraid, hoping he would be kind and gentle.

Hoag stood frozen, stunned by a woman so beautiful that she could not be real.

Lorena waited breathlessly for the romance, the gentle courting, that never came.

He walked toward her like a bull, forceful, demanding.

A short time later, she sat battered and alone on the edge of the bed.

Downstairs, Hoag, having failed his desire and back in his britches, charged into the front room where a fire still burned. He bent down, stoked it, and added a chunk of wood. He grabbed a bottle of whiskey from the shelf and drank from it. He kept drinking. Sweat ran down his face. He slammed his fist against the mantle, grimaced at the pain, spun around, and looked back up the stairs.

Hoag went to his big chair, sat down, and kept drinking.

Days later at the Ramsey Ranch, nothing had changed.

Watching the house from the corral stood Spitz, a sixty-five-year-old foreman with a gray handlebar mustache. He was wearing chaps and a leather vest. Spitz left his horse saddled in the corral and came out, closing the gate. He looked worried. Having always ridden for the brand but now worried, he knew he couldn't hold back much longer.

Alongside him, Luke, a young cowboy with freckles, held a lariat. They stood next to the corral fence. Luke's bay gelding was pawing dirt.

They could hear Hoag's loud, roaring voice from the big house but were unable to make out the words.

"Geez," Luke said, "ever since they got here, he's been yelling and throwing stuff around. Must be drunk again. And out of his head. Who's going to protect her?"

Spitz folded his arms, grimaced, but didn't respond.

Luke was nervous. "Do you think she's going to be all right? Her and the boy?"

Spitz tugged at his hat brim. "I'll send one of the men to the Bar Seven so he can tell Mrs. Ramsey I said she'd best come on home."

The rage from the house abruptly fell into eerie silence.

Spitz took a chaw of hard tobacco and leaned on the fence. An old-timer who had deep respect for women and disgust for drunks, Spitz wasn't sure what to do. Unarmed, he glanced toward a rifle leaning near the open door of the nearby tack room.

From the house, Hoag's voice rose again like thunder, echoing to the world outside.

Inside the house, a fire still burned in the big stone hearth in the front room.

Over the mantle hung a '73 Winchester repeater. On a hook to the left of the fireplace dangled Hoag's gun belt with his always-loaded, single-action Colt.

Hoag, barefoot and rattled from heavy drinking, paced the room. His blue shirt wet from liquor, his britches sagging, he looked dirty and dangerous.

His new bride, Lorena, walked in with in a tray of coffee. Ever graceful and shapely in her print dress, her long, golden hair done up and away from her face, no woman could be more beautiful. Fearful and upset, she was trying hard to appease him.

She had made a bargain and had said her vows but was now only miserable. The handsome gentleman who had found her in Kansas wasn't here; instead, she was facing a mean drunk.

She drew a deep breath, hoping to make a difference.

"Please, Hoag, have some coffee. You'll feel better."

She set the tray on a table near the sofa.

"I ain't never had no trouble afore I got you," he snarled.

He watched her and wet his lips, too drunk to think clearly.

He walked over as she held up a cup of coffee. He knocked it from her hand.

The cup sailed through the air with coffee flying, then crashed against the rock hearth. It made a loud, shattering noise. She looked afraid but determined.

The sound brought her son Asa. Fully dressed, he hurried from another room to pause some ten feet behind Hoag, who didn't see him.

Hoag, unaware of the boy, faced Lorena. His wild eyes reflected how drunk he was. He squinted, narrowing his gaze. His mouth went sideways. He staggered.

Lorena, unable to escape around him, forced a smile and touched his arm. He brushed her hand away.

"It's all your fault," Hoag snarled. "And that blasted kid."

Lorena winced. "You said you liked Asa. You said a lot of nice things back in Kansas."

"He's going to talk right now, or I'll beat it out of him."

Hoag followed her gaze, turning to see Asa standing in the doorway.

Lorena hurried around Hoag to block his path. Their gazes locked.

Hoag growled in full rage. "Get out of my way."

"Leave him alone."

"You've been asking for it."

Hoag slammed the back of his hand across her cheek, knocking her back a few steps. Stunned, she staggered and fought for balance. Asa ran around her.

Asa charged Hoag, pounding him.

Hoag laughed and knocked the boy down with his fists. Hoag kicked at the fallen boy, his boot stunning and dazing Asa's meager defense.

Lorena backed to the fireplace, spun, and grabbed a poker before coming forward.

"Don't you touch him!"

LEE MARTIN

Hoag turned in fury, hit her on the arm, and seized the poker from her hand. He shoved her back and beat her across the face and shoulders with his other fist.

Hoag, still holding the poker in his right hand, forced her to the floor with his left. He kicked her, twice. She cried out and tried to roll clear, but he kept at it.

She struggled to rise. He kicked her harder.

She rolled back on the floor in pain, still determined but badly damaged.

Hoag paused. Despite his drunken rage, he had to admire her courage. But she was too darn beautiful, so much so he hesitated to even embrace her. He had suffered for this; it made him feel as if he were less than a man and unable to be a husband to a goddess.

On the floor, a stunned Asa tried to get up.

Hoag turned from the fallen Lorena. He kicked Asa on the shoulder, beating him back to the floor. He threatened him with the poker but didn't use it.

Hoag growled at the boy. "Now you talk!"

Asa got to one knee. Hoag kicked the boy's arms protecting his chest, knocking him back down again. Asa gasped for air.

Lorena managed to get to her feet. She staggered over and grabbed Hoag's arm. He swung back at her, knocking her down, sending her sliding across the floor and almost into the hearth.

Hoag turned back to kicking Asa.

The boy covered his face and head with his arms.

Hoag kept on kicking him. "Yell, blast you!"

Hoag balanced the poker as he hovered over the boy. He raised it high as he staggered a little, preparing to bring it down on Asa's head.

Lorena got to her feet and turned to the hanging gun belt. She grabbed the Colt, yanked it free, pulled the hammer back, and turned. She stumbled around behind the fallen boy and faced Hoag.

"Stop or I'll shoot!"

Hoag lowered the poker in surprise, then ignored her as he snorted and raised the poker to slam it down on the boy's head.

"Talk, you little brat!"

30

As Hoag started his swing, she fired.

Catching the bullet in his chest, poker still in hand, Hoag stared at her in disbelief. His eyes went round, wild. Drunk as he was, he knew he was dying before he hit the floor. He dropped to his knees and grabbed at his chest.

Lorena stood transfixed with the revolver in both hands.

Her eyes wide with horror, she swayed.

Hoag went down and rolled on his side, a dead man.

Lorena hurried to Asa as the boy sat up and reached for her.

⟞⟝

The following night, Elk Creek, shivering with a freeze, seemed quiet. A few horses waited at rails near the saloon. A wagon without a team remained in front of the closed general store. No one was in sight.

Sam rode toward the faded jailhouse on his right. A lamp burned by the door. On either side of the jail's front windows, standing away from the light on the boardwalk, two rough-looking Ramsey gunmen waited. They wore heavy coats pulled back from their sidearms.

Crowe, on the left, had beady eyes fixed on Sam.

Crenshaw, wearing his fancy boots, stood on the right.

Sam recognized them. He reined up at the hitching rail but did not move as they came forward on the boardwalk. Moonlight hit their crude faces. Hands at their holsters, they looked menacing.

Crowe spat to the side. "That's close enough, Jeffries."

Sam looked from one to the other. He saw a crack of light from inside the jail as someone peered out through a shuttered window.

Crowe sneered. "Don't push your luck."

"You got no business here," Crenshaw said.

Sam dismounted slowly. He draped the reins around the hitching rail. His eyes piercing and deadly, he let it show he had no use for the Ramseys or their hired guns. Sam moved around the railing.

The two men backed to either side of the jail's entrance.

Sam walked up to the jail door. He waited.

The two bad men looked at each other. Sweat beaded on their faces.

Now Crowe, eyes wild, slowly lowered his right hand to his Colt and rested his hand on the weapon.

Sam, his back to Crowe, knocked on the door.

Crenshaw moved aside, waiting for Crowe.

The door opened a crack.

Crowe suddenly drew. Sam spun at the click as his Colt leaped in his hand. Crowe fired and missed. Sam's bullet slammed into Crowe's chest. Sam fanned the hammer and turned, ready for Crenshaw.

Crowe, doubled up, staggered backward and into the street. Crowe grabbed his chest, blood running through his fingers, and dropped to his knees.

Frozen, Crenshaw worked his lips. Sweat dribbled off his nose.

Sam still held his Colt, ready to fire again.

Crenshaw moved sideways and into the street, where he grabbed Crowe's arm. He tried to pull him up as they moved away, but Crowe dropped dead in the dirt.

Crenshaw turned to glare up at Sam. "The Ramseys ain't going to like this."

Crenshaw backed away, hurried off to the other side of the street, pushing through the curious crowd emerging from the saloon, and went inside.

Sam holstered his Colt and turned around as the jailhouse door opened.

⬦⬦

Inside the Elk Creek jailhouse, Sheriff Tyree closed and barred the door behind Sam after he entered. A hot fire in the iron stove kept it warm inside. At the back of the room, a closed door hid the cells.

Tyree walked back to his desk and stood behind it. He pushed his hat back, drawing a deep breath. "It took you long enough."

"A little trouble with Crowe. He's dead."

"I know."

"So you just watched?"

"I figured you could handle it."

Sam looked around the office. "What's so all-fired important, dragging me out here in the middle of the night? We're supposed to go hunting tomorrow, remember? Not that you can hit anything, the way you're getting so hitched up. You'll be sitting in camp half the time. I may have to carry you around."

"Yeah, sure, that'll be the day."

Sam walked over to the stove where he helped himself to some thick coffee in a cracked cup. The coffee smelled horrible, but that would never stop Sam, who had tasted and smelled a lot worse in the war and on the cattle trail.

Tyree sat at his desk. "I got a bad situation on my hands."

Sam turned, sipping the coffee, and grimaced at the taste of it.

"How some ever, you keep killing off the Ramsey guns, it'll improve some." Tyree pushed his hat back. "But I need your help."

Sam walked over to the window and turned but didn't sit down.

"Are we going hunting or not?" Sam asked.

The sheriff leaned forward, hands on the desk. He fiddled with a stack of reward posters, making them neat. Then he leaned back and looked up at Sam.

"You're not listening, Sam, as usual. Now I've got a deal for you, and you can use the money to start up your place." He paused for effect. "Five hundred dollars."

Impressed but suspicious, Sam pushed his hat back from his lined brow.

Tyree stood up and nodded toward the cells behind the closed door.

"Maybe you'd better have a look."

Sam made a face before setting his cup down. Tyree turned and walked to the closed door to the cells. Tyree opened the door.

Sam followed as they walked inside to the three cells, one of which was empty.

In the first cell lay an old man, sound asleep in an awkward position on the bunk, a silly smile on his thin, unshaven face. He was a grubby and decrepit mule skinner.

Tyree gestured. "Lester, still fighting Comanches."

In the second cell, also unlocked, sat Lorena Ramsey with her back to them. A blue cape covered her riding clothes, and her boots protruded from under her skirts. Her hair was long and shining in the pale lamplight. She didn't turn.

Sitting at her side and gazing at Sam, young Asa had wild eyes. He wore a heavy coat. His face was black and blue; the boy had been beaten severely. Two carpet bags sat next to them.

Sam could not look at the damage and turned, leaving the cell area.

Tyree followed, closing the door behind them.

"Hoag beat them pretty bad," Tyree said.

Tyree walked to the front window and peered into the street through a crack in the shutters, then returned to his desk. He stood behind it.

Sam picked up his coffee cup, went to the stove, and poured himself more coffee.

Tyree continued. "Seems the boy won't talk since his pa died, something like five years ago. She thought if she remarried, he'd have another father, and it would help some. But no such luck."

Sam turned, sipped the bad coffee, and tried not to react, but what he had seen in the cell grated on him.

Tyree grimaced. "Late this afternoon, Hoag got drunk, beat her up, and then went after the boy with a poker."

Sam waited for the rest of it.

"She shot him dead."

"That's no loss," Sam said. He returned his cup to the table by the stove and left it.

Tyree sat on the edge of his desk. "Being as there's no law in Red Hat, the foreman Spitz and young Luke brung them here by wagon. Seems Ike and his two other sons are off on a drive. Ike's wife Emma had been staying at a neighbor's, but she must have come back. I figure that's why Crowe and Crenshaw showed up. They made a lot of noise over at the saloon—trying to drum up a hanging."

Sam made a face as he listened to Tyree.

"Emma Ramsey's a hard woman and her favorite little boy was shot dead. She won't rest until his widow is dangling from some tree. You can bet on it.

But Spitz signed an affidavit and said he'd testify on their behalf, if it came to that. He and Luke took off afore the Ramseys could get to them."

Sam took it all in as he turned to warm his hands.

"They're both hurt bad. Can hardly walk," Tyree said. "It was self-defense, Sam, an excusable homicide to save her son. Nobody could say different."

Sam adjusted his gun belt. He digested the information.

Tyree stood. "But if we don't get them out of here, Emma will hang her for sure. It would take an army to hold them off. I don't have one. Everyone's afraid of the Ramseys."

"Take her up to Salt Lake. You can put her on the train back to Kansas."

Tyree walked around his desk and sat down.

"Ike's spread covers a good half of this whole country. He's got over fifty men, and I figure they're already blocking the main trails by now. Especially north."

Sam looked reluctant, so Tyree continued with a little more pressure.

"That's a real pretty woman. I need someone I can trust. To make sure no harm comes to her along the way. Somebody who ain't afraid of Ramsey."

Sam began to pace and went back to sipping his coffee.

"I know how you feel about women, Sam, but she needs help."

"You know Ramsey's just itching to get me out of Colorado."

"You can take care of yourself. It's the woman and boy we got to think about."

Tyree stood, walked around to the wall map of the territory and surrounding areas. He ran his finger across it.

"I got the word out that she'd be taken north to Salt Lake. If you go west, you'd find them waiting, but they know you wouldn't go crossing the desert. To the east, snow could block you in the passes. I don't figure they're bothering much south of town because nobody'd be crazy enough to try to cross the Grand River this time of year. And even if you got across, there's the badlands farther south. That's outlaw country. Maybe some stray Apaches, but Geronimo's been arrested and gone back to the San Carlos reservation."

Sam considered Tyree's words, but he knew Geronimo would not stay put. The trick would be to move fast, just in case.

Tyree continued. "I'll have some men follow you all the way down to Grand River. They say there's an old raft; it might be in one piece still. At Bell's Crossing. The river will be pretty high now, but one way or the other, they'll help you get across with ropes and whatever else they can rig. Once you're over it, they'll lead a false trail west on the north side of the river and then double back."

Sam walked closer to the map. Tyree pointed to lines running south through the mesa and red cliff country.

"Army has a camp about here on the San Juan. You'll carry a letter from me, so they'll give you escort down through New Mexico Territory. You can pick up transport and take her south into Texas, where she's got some brothers in the rangers."

The sheriff returned to sit on the edge of his desk.

"I know you been down through some of that country."

"No place for a woman and a boy."

"Chances are, you won't find no trouble. Besides, once you make the San Juan, you'll have the army. And Lester, he's been there. And my deputy. Now we got no woman's saddle, but I figure she won't care."

"Deputy?"

"An old friend I sent for. He used to scout down there. "

Sam waited uneasily.

"And one more. Fellow named Silas Parker. She met him on the stage. Seems to be impressed with him. He gets two hundred for going along."

Sam grimaced. "Parker? He'd sell his own mother for gambling stakes."

"He don't much like you neither. But that's all I got. And Parker already knows you're in charge."

"How much time do I have?"

"None. I figure Ike Ramsey'll be here anytime soon." Tyree adjusted his hat. "But I got your outfits all ready, so we won't waste no time."

Tapping at the door caught their attention.

Tyree walked over, peered through the hole in the door and opened it.

In walked Ezra Hawkins, bearded and wild eyed. At eighty, he was a little bent over and lame. A deputy badge dangled from his leather vest. He wore range clothes and a fringed-buckskin jacket. He appeared unlikely to be able to mount a horse.

Hawkins carried a Sharps rifle, fit more for buffalo than the badlands.

Tyree grinned. "Sam Jeffries. Ezra Hawkins."

Hawkins and Sam shook hands, gingerly.

Sam looked the crippled old man over and shook his head.

He turned to Tyree. "You're going to get me killed."

"You've been trying that for a long time."

Hawkins took offense. "You never mind, sonny. I can outride you any day. And, yeah, maybe I can whup you too."

"Where's Parker?" Tyree asked Hawkins.

"Out back with the horses."

"Wait here," Tyree said to Hawkins.

Sam followed Tyree through the door to the back cells.

Tyree walked into Lester's cell and shook him gently.

Lester sat up, reaching for his six-gun, but saw Tyree and grinned. Lester yawned, then saw Sam outside the cell.

"Hey, Sam," Lester said.

Tyree walked out and around, opened Lorena's cell door.

Her back to them, she turned slowly. The boy held her hand. Her face, badly bruised, had no expression. She and Asa stood up, both barely able to walk.

Her heavy blue cape parted to show a satin purse tight at her waist. Asa dragged his left foot. She limped, unsteady. They came out of the cell.

"Mrs. Ramsey, this here's Sam Jeffries. You've already met Hawkins and Lester."

Sam expected to see a miserable, grieving woman. Instead, he saw a fierce defiance—the fury of a mother protecting her son. Despite himself, he had to admire her for that reason.

Asa looked up at Sam as their knight.

The men followed Lorena and Asa to the front office. She stopped by the desk, not moving for a long moment. She leaned in it.

"She'll pay all of you in Texas," Tyree said.

Sam, on the spot, knew what he had to do. "Don't want no money, but I'm making the rules."

Lorena, startled that he would not take pay for helping her, calmed herself. She didn't understand a man like Sam, but her respect was growing by the minute.

Sam spoke directly to her and the boy. "If you want to stay alive, you'll do as I say. At all times. Agreed?"

Hurt and angry, she hesitated only a moment. At length, she nodded as her son took her hand.

Tyree went around his desk and pulled open a drawer. "Hold on a minute, Sam."

Tyree, after pulling out an old spyglass, came around and handed it to Sam along with the letter. "My pa had this when he was at sea. You get to the badlands, you're going to need it."

"It ain't right."

"Let me figure what's right. Besides, we're going to be partners when I hang up this badge, so I'll get it back. Now, come on. I'll walk you to the alley."

Sam fondled the spyglass.

Chapter 3

The next evening at the Ramseys' ranch, Ike Ramsey, his two sons, and a dozen hands returned from a cattle drive up north. Cold, weary, sweaty, and hungry, they headed for home. Shadows were long. The sun's remaining glow hung low at the horizon.

Harley and Jonas lagged far behind and reined up on the ridge. They watched from a quarter mile away as Ike and the hands rode to the corrals.

Jonas hated the sudden memory of another ridge: four years ago, he had been riding on it when he looked down and saw his father, brothers, and hired guns raiding and murdering at the Madison shirttail spread. He still had nightmares. He wanted to get away from here, but Harley had been ignoring his question.

Jonas persisted. "So what do you think?"

Harley didn't answer but grinned at the scene below. "Pa's sure in a hurry. He hates being away from Ma. I ain't never letting no woman get a hold of me like that."

"So he loves her," Jonas said, wondering why the fuss.

"You don't even know the half of it. Long before you came along, Ma made a trip to Cheyenne to see her mother before she died."

"Wait, she has kin?"

"I was about eight and Hoag a few years older, but I sure remember. Pa near went loco without her. Couldn't even sleep in their bed. Camped out by the fireplace. I'd get up and peek out and he'd be rolling around."

"He could have gone with her."

"He'd have been run off or shot." Harley waved his hand at the country-side. "When they eloped, her family cut her off."

"I didn't know."

"You wasn't even born, but seeing Pa just now in such a hurry, it brought some of it back." Harley tugged at his hat brim. "But don't you ever say anything about her having kin. We ain't supposed to know."

Jonas pushed his hat back as they rode down the ridge.

"Okay," Harley said, "now to get back to your question. Yeah, you had your fancy schooling, but forget about joining the army."

"I could go in as a lieutenant."

"Ma wants all her chicks in the nest." Harley said. "When Hoag and I got back from the War, she made sure we were all partners on the deed with her and Pa. She wanted us to stay put." Harley paused to grin. "Except she never expected Hoag to marry a woman like that."

"Like what?"

Harley chuckles. "Gorgeous, that's what."

"I like her. And the boy."

"Yeah but with all of us on the deed, the way it's written, if anything happens to Hoag, his wife gets his share." Harley pushed his hat back and grinned. "In that case, Ma would probably shoot her."

Jonas nodded but didn't think the comments were laughable. Not after what he had seen at the Madison spread.

Joining the army would have taken Jonas into another world. He did not rule it out, but for now he would just consider the option. If he chose to leave, it would have to be without any notice, just a letter left behind.

Harley and Jonas caught up with their father. They dismounted and turned their horses into the corral for the hands to unsaddle, water, and feed.

Ike looked angry. "Something's wrong."

Night air, cold and miserable, drove them toward the lamplight in the ranch house.

"Spitz plumb disappeared," Ike said. "Best foreman I ever had."

"Sure ain't like him," Harley said.

"And Luke went with him. They took their gear and lit out."

Harley shrugged. "Luke was okay, but he was just a kid anyhow."

Ike and his two sons, wearing heavy coats, walked side by side in the dark.

Ike Ramsey limped from a long-ago fall from a horse. He spat tobacco juice and looked meaner than sin. A white scar on his left cheek leaned into new lines dragging his mouth down at the corners

Ike feared no one, except his wife Emma, but only because he could not be without her. Since he had first seen her at a dance in Cheyenne, he had been lost in love for her. He let her run rough shod over all of them rather than fight with her.

Harley and Jonas had learned to never back-sass their father and, more importantly, to never give their mother one speck of argument.

Ike spat out the last of the tobacco juice and wiped his mouth with his bandana. He was never allowed to chew and spit in the house, but he didn't mind.

Waiting on the porch with an apron over her print dress, Emma Ramsey could convince anyone the devil was really female. A handsome woman, caring wife, and loyal mother, she had also become a vicious woman ready for revenge. They could see her anger burning in her face and gaze.

Ike limped up to her, gave her a kiss on the cheek, but paused to stare at her fury.

She gathered them inside the warm house. The three men closed and barred the door behind them, then moved to the fireside and stood helpless.

Emma drew herself up. "Hoag's dead and buried on the hillside."

Harley stepped back. "What?"

Emma's anger reddened her face. "And she done it, that precious wife of his."

Jonas and Ike, both stunned, stood speechless.

Harley shook his head. "I don't get it, how could…"

"Two days ago, Hoag was drinking, but never mind that." Emma said. "I sent Crowe and Crenshaw after her, soon's I got back. All the way to Elk Creek. But Crowe got killed. Day before yesterday."

Ike, shattered by the loss of a son, turned his face away.

"Who got Crowe?" Harley asked.

Emma paused for effect, then answered. "Sam Jeffries."

Ike growled, his back to them.

"Where is she now?" Harley asked.

"I don't know," Emma said, "but she's not getting away with it."

Jonas went to stand with his father in front of the hearth.

Harley fell silent under her glare.

❖

Later that night in the Ramseys' ranch house, Emma stormed around the supper table like a clucking hen. A fire was blazing in the hearth.

Jonas and Harley finished their meal and received more coffee from Emma, who could not still herself for one moment. She cleaned off the table as Ike got up and walked to the fireside.

Ike, his back to them and ready to explode, stared at the crackling wood and flames.

Emma brought more coffee to Ike, who remained silent.

Jonas and Harley stayed at the table to clean and oil their pistols, then their rifles.

No one spoke for a long while, not until the weapons were clean.

Emma stood at Ike's side as he sat staring into the hearth.

"Don't worry, Ma," Harley said, putting his rifle on the wall rack. "She's probably locked up in jail."

Emma shook her head. "The boys heard how Spitz told the sheriff it was self-defense. That Hoag got drunk and beat her and the boy."

Harley stood up by the table. "So that's why he split."

Emma walked to the mantle and slammed her fist down. The clock bounced. "I want her hanged. And we can't leave any witnesses."

Jonas, who seldom argued with anyone, straightened. "Ma, you can't do that."

Harley looked at his furious mother and kept his mouth shut.

Jonas had liked Lorena and the boy. He wanted nothing to do with tracking them down, but he had to do something. He couldn't help her if he stayed behind. He stood up alongside Harley.

Emma ignored Jonas and continued. "Crenshaw heard they were taking her up to Salt Lake, where the army could get them on a train. So I sent some of the men to block the trail and some to block the trail east, but the passes will be closed. Even if they chanced the deserts to the west, they'd run into our outriders just the same."

"What about south?" Harley asked.

Emma shook her head. "Some of the men will ride as far south as Grand River, but in this time of year, there is no chance of getting across it, even at Bell's Crossing. And even then, nobody in their right mind would keep going south to the badlands, not with a woman and a boy."

"Who's taking her?" Harley persisted.

"Sam Jeffries."

Ike's right fist clinched on the chair arm as he kept staring into the flames. Sam Jeffries had been wearing a badge when he had killed Ike's brother two years ago. Ike harbored a hatred for Sam that could only be satisfied if Sam were dead. Getting Sam out of Colorado might be Ike's chance—Lacey's badge would be a long ways away.

Harley slid his six-gun down into his holster. "He don't scare me none."

Emma's gaze darkened, growing crazier by the minute. "My first-born is *dead*."

Harley took offense. "You still got us."

"Yes, but you, Harley," she said, "you gamble too much. Sometimes you stink of perfume from those painted women. At least Hoag got married. He tried to do right."

Harley sat back down. "Hoag wasn't perfect. He could be real mean."

"But he's the one I lost," she countered.

"Well," Harley said, "they could be dragging her back here real soon."

She shook her head. "We should have heard by now, so we can't wait any longer."

Ike stood up slowly. He had not been that fond of Hoag, and he had more on his mind than a fugitive woman.

"It's Sam Jeffries I want to hang," Ike said, slowly turning. "At daybreak, we head for Elk Creek."

"And I'm going with you," Emma said.

Harley shook his head. "Ma, you can't sit in a sidesaddle for as long as it might take us. Your legs would fall off."

"I'm riding Hoag's saddle. He'd want it that way."

The others stared at her, but her fire outshone theirs. Even Ike just nodded.

⊰⊱

Later that night, while Jonas and Harley were asleep in their rooms, Emma stood next to Ike in front of the fire. He put his arm around her and drew her close, the way he liked her to be.

Emma rested her head on his shoulder. "When we put our sons on the deed, we never expected this, and I'll never let her make a claim."

They were silent a moment. Emma knew how soft hearted he could be, so she didn't push him about Lorena. She'd handle it when they caught up with her. Whatever happened, Emma could never allow Lorena to claim Hoag's share of the ranch.

"Maybe," she said, "we should leave Jonas here to run things."

"We've got a good ramrod. Besides, if we leave him behind, he might go running off to see that Madison girl. He likes her, but all she wants is to find out who killed her folks."

"But Jonas doesn't know anything about it."

"Maybe not, but we gotta keep 'em apart." Ike grimaced. "Jonas is a good hand with a rope. He can ride any bronc you throw at him. And he's a better shot than any of us, but he ain't like us."

Emma did not respond.

"And I'm still trying to make a man out of him. It's time he stood alongside us."

Emma remained silent in the circle of his arm.

"After all," Ike added, "he's still my son."

Ike leaned down to kiss her cheek, then headed toward the bedroom.

Emma hesitated as she watched him leave, then made a face as she stared into the fire.

Daybreak, far south of Elk Creek, fell on rugged land with snow patches and red sandstone cliffs, where dwarf juniper and scraggly brush hid little varmints.

Overcast, cold, windy.

Sam, Hawkins, Lester, Lorena Ramsey, Parker, and the boy rode southwest. They were dressed warm yet felt every bit of the icy wind.

Some distance behind them, four of the sheriff's deputies, leading two pack mules loaded with ropes and harnesses, rode directly in their tracks with a plan to divert their trail at Grand River.

Lorena rode astride her horse, her cape and skirts piled up behind her and barely covering her boot tops. Asa rode on her left; Parker, on her right. The slick gambler paid her a great deal of attention.

Right behind them and ahead of the deputies, Lester led two packhorses.

In the far lead, Sam and Hawkins scouted the trail.

Hawkins looked back over his shoulder. "That poor girl is hurt so bad she can hardly sit in the saddle." He spat. "And I sure don't like the way that Parker keeps looking at her."

Sam agreed in silence.

The wind began to rise. They bent low in the saddle. They had a sense of being watched, of danger about to land on them.

Rising wind whistled in the trees, saddles creaked, and horses' hooves hit the hard ground like hammers. The smell of leather and horse sweat seemed more intense, mingling with the stink of rabbit brush along the way.

The sky began to darken with fast-moving clouds.
Sam looked up and sniffed the coming rain.

⚉

Late in the day, heavy rain drenched Sam and his party as they fought their way over and through red sandstone mounds and wound down the trail to the rushing Little Cross Creek.

Night fell as they reined up. All wore slickers, but the cold and wet still got to their faces and chilled them to the bone. They rode stiff and hunched over.

Little Cross Creek, musical and wide with a fast-moving current, looked shallow. A few stray cottonwoods and willows with green, lance-shaped leaves lined the south bank with serviceberry and chokecherry bushes beaten down by the pounding rain.

To the east, a dark and snow-striped forest covered the foothills below the white crests of the Rockies. The overcast sky allowed an eerie touch of sunlight to creep through and guide them.

Despite the storms, the pretty creek caused everyone but Parker to envision a house on the nearby rise with cattle and horses grazing beyond.

Sam and Hawkins led the way south across the creek. Parker, Lorena, and her son rode behind them. Lester followed with the packhorses.

Their mounts fought the rain and busy current. Lorena and her son, still suffering from their injuries, could barely stay in the saddle, but they all made it to the south bank.

The sheriff's four men soon appeared and crossed with their pack mules.

"Maybe the rain will cover our tracks," Hawkins said to Sam.

"If it keeps up."

They continued south with Sam leading the way.

Hawkins brought up the rear just behind the four deputies, who followed Lester and the packhorses.

Lorena, Asa, and Parker fought to keep up with Sam.

The rain fell so heavily that their mounts struggled.

The storm muffled their voices.

Lorena rode up alongside Sam. "Mr. Parker said there could be outlaws where we're going. And Apaches. He said once we reach Grand River, we should go east. Is he right?"

Sam grunted but shook his head.

Annoyed with Sam's indifference, she fell back beside Parker.

"He doesn't like me," she said to Parker.

"He doesn't like anyone. But don't worry, ma'am. I'll look after you and the boy, and unlike Jeffries, I'm not doing it just for the money."

Lorena wondered whether he meant chivalry or something less admirable.

She had lost her first and only love in a wagon accident. If not for Asa, she may not have married again. Now she knew it had been folly to trust Hoag. She had learned her lesson—trust no man.

She wasn't listening to Parker's rhetoric. Instead, she was watching Sam far ahead. She didn't trust him either, but there was something about Sam that commanded respect.

As night fell, Sam led them to high but rocky ground where they would not only make camp to avoid flash floods but also find a better view.

⊰⊱

Later, the overhanging rocks and inclines offered Sam's camp on higher ground some shelter from the rain flooding the area. Battered bushes and clumped junipers lined the terrain both around and below them.

With two tarps providing partial cover, they huddled around a campfire.

The deputies made their own camp on a nearby rise with tarps.

At daybreak, Sam stood on the higher terrain, out of earshot, rifle in hand. He huddled in his slicker as water poured off his hat's brim. Lester took shelter with the horses farther away. Parker slept under an overhanging rock near the fire pit.

Under the tarp, Hawkins sat up in his blankets. He rubbed his eyes and saw Lorena shaking the coffee pot over the flames in the fire pit near him. She had a blanket around her. She shivered, numb from the chill.

The tarp kept them mostly dry, but the storm continued noisy and wet around them. Near her, Asa slept soundly. They could see the deputies' campfire shielded by rocks and tarps on the nearby rise.

Hawkins, blanket wrapped around him, warmed his hands. Chilled and stiff all over, he could only move slowly and deliberately. Lorena's movements, because of her injuries, were almost as slow as his.

"Coffee smells good," he said.

She poured the steaming coffee into two cups. She handed him one.

"Do you think we can get across the big river?" she asked.

"One of the deputies has a swimming horse. They say they got it all figured out."

"A swimming horse?"

"Ain't many of 'em can handle a river."

She thought about it as she held her cup in both hands.

"So where are you from, Mr. Hawkins?"

"The Rocky Mountains mostly. I spent my foolish years trapping beaver. Got married three times to Ute women and widowed three times."

"I'm sorry. No children?"

"Five of 'em, but the Utes said I was bad luck and chased me out of their part of the Rockies." He paused to sip his coffee. "I got roped into being a scout for the army until I was too stoved up to do any good."

She held her cup in both hands, drinking slowly as he continued.

"Then I got word from Sheriff Tyree on account of we rode together once. When I heard about the spot you were in, I figured you needed me."

Lorena smiled her thanks and fondled her cup as rain poured off the tarp and spat the ground around them. Lightning flashed far off in the flats. Lorena worried Asa would awaken; storms often frightened him.

Hawkins nodded toward the sleeping Asa.

"I guess he never got over losing his real pa. How'd that happen?"

Lorena liked the old man and wanted him to know. "Five years ago in a storm like this. He was bringing Asa home from school. The wagon overturned on a grade, and my husband was killed in the tumble. Asa was only five, but he stayed with his father all night under the wagon. Ever since, Asa won't say a word. And he cannot be alone when there's a bad storm. I'm just glad he's sleeping so well."

Hawkins gave her a kindly look.

She straightened. "What about Lester?"

"Ain't been the same since the Comanches got him a long time ago down in Texas. Been a little crazy ever since, but you can count on him, whatever comes. He's still a tough hombre."

Hawkins stood and stretched his weary bones before sitting back down to enjoy his coffee.

Lorena looked at Parker sleeping farther away.

"Mr. Parker seems like a gentleman."

"I wouldn't trust him as far as I could throw a rattler."

Lorena glanced toward Sam, who stood like a statue far off in the rain.

"Mr. Jeffries acts like a bear and looks so mean all the time. Does he hate everybody?"

"Ramseys for sure. When he had a badge, Sam was plumb sure they was killing squatters, but he couldn't prove it. Then Tyree said Sam killed Ike's brother Joe in a gunfight." Hawkins sipped his coffee. "Oh, Joe started it, but Ike would sure like to get even."

"I didn't know."

"And Sam, he don't like women much."

She stood to shake out her blanket, wrapping it around her before sitting down again.

Hawkins spoke more softly, for her ears only.

"Tyree says Jeffries was in the army for a time. The cavalry. Worked his way up the ranks to lieutenant. Got married. She didn't like the army because there never was enough pay to buy the things she wanted, so he mustered out."

Lorena listened, more than interested.

Hawkins continued. "Then Lacey, a US marshal, he pinned a badge on Sam, who needed work to support his wife. She didn't like the badge either."

Lorena moved a little closer, intent on the rest.

Hawkins settled back a little and shook his head.

"Sam's been shot up a couple dozen times. Carries a lot of lead in him. Like me, I reckon. He was hoping to earn enough with a badge to get himself a spread of his own and raise a family. But she didn't like that on account of she wasn't living on no dirty, old ranch."

"So what happened?"

"She ran off with another fellah, but their wagon got ran off a cliff. Both got killed."

"That's so sad."

Hawkins nodded. "Tyree said that as the road had so many prints, no one could tell who was there at the time. Folks still think Sam done it."

"Do you?"

"All I know is a woman can make any man crazy." He glanced at her. "And she had yeller hair. Only she weren't near as pretty as you."

Lorena blushed, but now she understood Sam a little more.

"After that, he went kind of wild. Got into all kinds of fights. And that's how he lost his badge."

"He didn't do it," she said.

"What?"

"He didn't kill his wife."

Hawkins, touched by her faith in Sam, could only smile. "What about you, ma'am? Got a heap of family?"

"Just my brothers in Texas," she said. "I'll be so glad to see them."

"Tough fellahs, huh?"

She nodded. "They're rangers. And a lot like Mr. Jeffries."

⊰⊱

The next morning, back in Elk Creek, rain fell heavy in the muddy street. In his office, Sheriff Tyree sat behind his desk with a shotgun resting on it. He glanced at his watch, waiting for the explosion sure to come from the Ramseys. He pushed his hat back from his brow. He leaned forward, his hand near the shotgun.

He heard riders outside at the railing.

Tyree, still seated, picked up the shotgun and aimed it at the door.

The jail front door slammed open.

Ike, wearing a heavy jacket, water running off his hat brim, stormed inside like the devil himself. Driven by Emma, he would at least put on a show; he knew she could hear through the open door.

Tyree looked unimpressed. He leaned forward.

Ike, red faced and furious, ignored the shotgun and slammed his fist on the desk.

"Where is she?"

"Hoag beat the heck out of her and her son. It was self-defense."

"I said, where is she?"

"On her way to Salt Lake City. The army will get 'em both on a train back to Kansas."

"Yeah, well, I got men out there, and she ain't showed up."

"Your men ain't too smart."

Ike fumed. "They won't get anywhere we can't find 'em."

"So what are you doing here?" The sheriff sat quietly, still holding the shotgun.

"Who's riding with 'em?" Ike demanded.

"Jeffries. Fellow named Parker. My deputy Ezra Hawkins."

"Crenshaw says Hawkins is just an old man."

"And Lester," Tyree added.

"A crazy, old fool."

"She shot Hoag to save her son. No court in the land would convict her. And you lay a hand on her, you'll be the one who hangs."

"I ain't forgetting you let her get away."

The sheriff stood with the shotgun aimed at Ike. "I'm warning you, Ike. You harm that woman, I'll track you down."

"I ain't scared of an old, beat-up sheriff."

"Maybe Emma's got it in for her, but it's Sam you're after."

"Jeffries got it coming."

"Listen to me, Ike. The days you was riding roughshod, they're about over. Railroads are coming west. Gonna send a spur through the black canyon and out to here."

Ike worked his mouth as Tyree kept needling him.

"And afore long, sheep are going to come this way." Tyree paused for effect, gesturing. "Why, before you know it, them little pointy hoofs and all them plows are going to be crossing over our graves. They won't even remember us."

"Now you listen to me, sheriff. This is my half of Colorado—I beat off the Injuns. Fought every bad winter and lost a heap of cattle and a lot of good men."

Ike paused to spit, spinning the spittoon, adjusted his hat, and continued.

"This is my land. No homesteaders. No stinking sheep. They come around here, they're in real trouble."

"Vigilante days are gone, Ike. You can't go around breaking the law."

"You can't stop me."

"I don't have to. I figure Jeffries has the Indian sign on you."

Ike straightened, sputtering. He looked ready to pull his Colt with his hand on his holster.

Instead, seeing the shotgun, Ike backed off and stormed out the office.

Tyree looked relieved and set down his shotgun. He moved to close and bar the door against the rain.

Outside the jail, Ike swung into the saddle among his sons and eleven armed men, including Corley and Crenshaw, as well as Emma. All had bedrolls, possible sacks and canteens. They wore slickers in the pouring rain.

Emma's fury reddened her face as she rode up beside Ike.

"We've been horn swaggled," Ike growled. "I figure they went south."

"No one can get across Grand River," Harley said.

Jonas reined closer. "Pa, when folks go down in the badlands, they ain't never heard from again."

Ike ignored him. "Anyone with a yellow belly can stay here."

"We're two days or more behind them," Jonas said.

"We'll catch up," Ike growled.

As Ike rode south, all followed in the rain.

—◄◘►—

On the red bluffs, Sam and his party reined up in the heavy rain. They looked down the grade at the cresting and tree-lined Grand River. Cottonwoods and junipers appeared black in the storm.

Like an out-of-control flood, the imposing and red-tinted river, with its vast width and powerful current, rushed southwest in terrifying strength. Only fools would consider any attempt to cross it, but Sam's party had no other choice.

"Dear God," Lorena whispered.

The four deputies came forward with their pack mules, which carried ropes and harnesses. Their hats drooped in the downpour.

They all followed Sam down the steep, barren trail to the river's edge.

Everyone was cold and wet, but none more so than Lorena and her son.

The old raft resting in the trees was in disrepair. They roped it tight, making it secure, but sensed no guarantees.

Trees on both sides allowed the deputies to set up a rope trail to bring over the raft, but they needed a rope on the other side.

One big deputy took it on himself to ride the current to the south side. He had a big roan, a swimming horse that could plow through the water. The deputy carried one end of a rope already shackled to a tree on the north side, where Sam's party waited.

Almost across, the deputy lost his horse to the river, but he swam the rest of the way with the rope and reached the far trees. His horse made it to shore farther down and came back along the south bank.

"Well, I'll be," Hawkins said.

As the day grew long, they now had three ropes across the river to bring Lorena and Asa over on the raft. They sat tucked inside the circle of supplies and gear.

Out on the raft in pouring rain, Lorena prayed as she and her son held on for dear life. Thrown about, they clung to the gear and supplies. Lorena's eyes closed often, but she remained brave for Asa's sake.

When the raft reached the south bank, the waiting deputy pulled them to safety.

The rest of the men swam their horses with ropes pulling and guiding them.

Before nightfall, Sam and his party were on the south bank.

The four deputies back on the north side kept their pack mules and used them to help lay a false trail west in the rain.

Sam waved his thanks as the deputies disappeared from view.

Pouring rain covered their tracks as Sam's party rode south from the river.

Sam and Hawkins led the way through a grove of tall aspens with green, restless leaves. They moved into the open and continued south. The others followed. They did not want to camp where they could be seen from the north side.

Hawkins rode over to Sam in the fading light.

"Ride due south. I'll catch up."

"What are you going to do?"

"Make sure we ain't followed."

"Watch yourself."

Hawkins reined up and turned back as Sam, Lorena, Asa, Parker, and Lester rode south up the red and yellow cliffs.

⁂

At the top of the rugged terrain in the darkening downpour, Sam and his party looked back at the wild Grand River. They turned to look south at a red-streaked land with deep canyons, white cliffs, scant trees, patches of snow, and no end in sight.

Lorena, soaked despite her slicker, shivered but worried over Asa.

Parker, aghast, could only grumble. "We're going to get lost."

Lester seemed to just take it all in stride.

Sam led the way across the red sandstone and onto high ground near the first deep canyon with black and red walls. Hawkins soon caught up with them with news that he had seen no one following.

A sudden roll of deafening thunder crossed the dark sky. They could not risk canyons because of flash floods, so they continued south.

Asa, eyes wide, rode closer to his mother. Again, a loud and terrifying roll of thunder—so loud even the horses shuddered—echoed and was followed by sparks of lightning that danced on the horizon.

Asa, pale and frightened by his memories, rode even closer to Lorena. Sam dropped back to ride on Asa's other side, keeping the boy between him and the grateful Lorena.

More horrifying thunder rolled through the clouds.

Lightning danced again along the cliffs.

Then came silence, followed by an even-darker sky and a burst of heavy rain. The downpour, so heavy it hurt the riders and their mounts, continued relentlessly.

The deluge continued for a long while, then diminished to just peaceful rainfall.

Sam led the way through the cliffs and onto the flats, where the land rolled to the far horizon. Only stray junipers and silver sage marked the red and endless landscape.

⧉

The rain had stopped to reveal occasional moonlight by the time Sam and his party reached an old adobe ruin out in the open. To the east, a huge flat mesa rose against the clearing sky.

The ruins appeared to have been a ranch house. The chimney was still standing over a partly caved-in roof. Walls stood about four feet high at most.

Lester settled the horses in one old room that had walls but no roof.

Under the half roof, Sam built a fire in the hearth with chips still smoking wet. The clear night and freezing cold forced everyone close to the flames. Lester took first watch on the perimeter.

Parker rolled up in his blankets and turned his back.

Lorena and Asa, barely able to eat beans, fell asleep as soon as they put their heads down. Hawkins added blankets to cover them and soon fell asleep near them.

Sam sat staring into the crackling fire. It smelled of dung but was hot and welcoming.

He forced himself to concentrate on how he might keep this amazing woman out of the hands of Emma Ramsey. As he stared into the flames, he knew Lacey was right. Sam hated himself for allowing his wife to have her way, something that could only happen when a man's a fool in love. Never again would he allow himself to weaken.

Sam looked into the flames and fell asleep, sitting with his rifle in hand.

Sometime during the night, Lorena turned over and saw Sam sound asleep with his rifle across his lap.

Only one other man in her life had inspired the admiration she felt for Sam. She had thought her late husband to be the best of men. She now thought of Sam in the same way.

⁂

Under a clear sky, Sam and his party left at daybreak, still heading south across a land of sudden canyons that often gave way to open stretches of short grass, silver sage, stunted junipers, and red earth that squished from the recent rain. To the far east rose the ever-present glory of distant mountains covered in snow.

Sam took the lead as usual. Lizards and a furry varmint scurried in the brush.

Parker, Lester with the packhorses, and Lorena and Asa followed in single file.

Trailing them, Hawkins kept an eye out for anyone behind them.

Lorena, still hurt from Hoag's beating, looked weary. Asa, bruised and sore, held up better than his mother because, as the man in the family, he had to protect her.

Lorena's admiration for Sam was not lost on Asa, and he fantasized about Sam being his father. He had accepted Hoag because his mother had needed to get away from Kansas and the grave where she had often wept for the last five years.

Asa worried as his mother struggled to stay astride.

Late in the day, Parker twisted in the saddle to look back and saw Lorena weaving.

Parker called out. "Jeffries, hold up!"

Sam turned his horse to ride back, just as Parker stopped Lorena from falling by grabbing her arm, forcing her upright in the saddle. She looked embarrassed.

Sam gestured toward the red bluffs not far to their left. He led them a few more miles and made camp under overhanging rocks in the hollow of a sandstone cliff. A few junipers and pinyon pine afforded additional shelter.

A little singing creek ran from the bluffs and disappeared in the red sand.

Darkness fell around them, but the sky remained clear as stars began to glitter. A lone coyote howled in the far distance, only once, and the silence remaining hung long into the night.

Hawkins stood guard on a nearby rise. Lester, having heated the beans and made the coffee, left to grain the horses.

Sam followed the creek into the bluffs to check his fish line.

Lorena and Asa, both weary and exhausted from their injuries and the hard ride, huddled by the fire as they ate beans. Asa didn't last long and soon was fast asleep in his blankets.

Parker, as always, fawned over Lorena, even as he poured her coffee.

Lorena, a little annoyed with the attention, turned to him.

"Mr. Jeffries has taken a particular dislike to you, Mr. Parker."

"Well, ma'am, he thinks I'm a tinhorn gambler."

"Are you?"

"No, ma'am, I'm a professional gambler. I used to travel the Mississippi on the riverboats. Made a good living." Parker smiled and leaned back. "Every kind of fool was ripe for the pickings. But it was more than that: the river was intoxicating. Hearing that whistle blow in the night...the lamplight on the black water..."

"So why did you leave?"

"Everybody was moving west to see the elephant. Big dreams. Stars in their eyes. Heading for a fall."

"And you?"

"Big dreams? Not until I boarded the stage and met you."

She got the message and sipped her coffee before looking away.

Parker continued. "I took one look at you, and my whole life turned up-side down. But you were taken."

Lorena, flattered but leery of him, stared into the fire.

Parker leaned back, resting his head on his saddle as he drew his blankets around him.

"But now everything's changed, and I plan to be first in line." Parker shifted in his blankets. "I'll keep Jeffries away from you—he's real crazy. They say he killed his own wife."

Lorena, annoyed, gave no response.

Parker persisted. "It's what folks believe. But don't you worry—I'll look after you. And maybe when this is over, you'll think about me in a better light. And San Francisco. They say the tall ships fill the harbor in a mist as soft as your golden hair."

Lorena had to admit she liked the image he was painting.

Parker opened his eyes, sat up as they heard someone coming.

Sam returned with four trout already cut, cleaned, and wrapped in mud. He placed them under the hot stones next to the fire. Then he got to his feet.

"A little late, aren't you?" Parker smirked.

"Fish for breakfast," Sam said. "Relieve Hawkins."

"Look here, Jeffries: it's too cold. And I'm getting real tired of being told what to do."

"If you'd do your job, I wouldn't have to bring it up."

Parker got to his feet, trying to look threatening. "Maybe we ought to make a few changes around here."

Sam, being taller than Parker, hovered over him. "Such as?" he asked.

Parker tried to stand taller. "You're so high and mighty, trying to impress the lady. Why don't you tell her how your wife ran off, and you—"

Sam's fist slammed into Parker's face. Stunned, Parker slid back from under the rock shelter, catching his balance as Sam approached.

Parker rushed him. They grappled, pounded each other at every chance. Boots slid in the dirt and brush.

They lost their footing and fell. They rolled toward the creek, bouncing off rocks. Parker kicked, grunting as they fought. Sam hit him hard on the jaw with his elbow. Parker clawed at Sam's eyes. Both men were sweaty and had blood on their faces.

Lorena, frantic, cried, "Please stop!"

They kept fighting. She put her hand over her mouth and turned away.

Sam and Parker hit the rocks by the creek. They broke apart, breathing hard, still prone.

Parker wiped blood from his nose with the back of his hand. They struggled to their knees. Parker got up first and kicked at Sam, who grabbed Parker's boot and twisted it. Parker fell on his rear with a thud. Sam twisted his boot again. Parker yelped.

Parker got free. Sam, now on his feet, slid sideways.

Parker, still on his knees, picked up a huge rock. He rose up, preparing to throw.

Sam ducked. The rock missed.

Sam pulled Parker to his feet and pounded the man's jaw with his fist until Parker gave up and dropped to his knees.

Sam growled at him. "Now relieve Hawkins."

A humiliated Parker stumbled to his feet; he turned and picked up his rifle. He headed for the rise and never looked back.

Sam wiped his bleeding mouth, hurting as bad as Parker, but was still in charge. He pulled his hat on and headed back to the camp.

Lorena and Asa pretended to be asleep in their blankets.

Sam built up the fire and sat down exhausted. He stared at Lorena and Asa.

Hawkins, relieved by Parker, came down from the rise for some coffee. He looked around at signs of the obvious disturbance.

"Don't ask, "Sam grunted as he checked the fish under the rocks.

"I seen it all," Hawkins said, grinning. He knelt down for the coffee.

Then the old man's humor sobered as he looked at Lorena.

"I got it figured out," Hawkins said. "Why Hoag got drunk and beat 'em."

Sam nodded, way ahead of him.

"Blaming her," Hawkins said, "when all the time, he probably was scared silly by the looks of her. Probably the only time he knew he was scum."

Lying with her eyes closed, Lorena felt her face turn hot. Hawkins had it right, she knew. Her thoughts were scrambled, but she could still see Hoag's face when he had left their bed on their wedding night at the ranch. Furious with self-ridicule, he had turned to the bottle, leaving her alone and shaken but grateful.

The marriage had never been consummated.

But before long, his drinking had turned into horror and disaster.

⚉

At day break farther north of Sam's path, Ike Ramsey, Emma astride in a heavy skirt, their two sons, and eleven men arrived on the north side of Little Cross Creek. They wore heavy coats. Their saddles were well packed.

They crossed easily under a clear sky.

The creek, lined with willows and cottonwoods, had its own music, but no one paid any heed. Only a need for revenge drove the Ramseys. Emma's anger remained the most dangerous. Ike wanted justice for his brother and his son, but to him, hanging a woman didn't sit right, even as he chose not to disagree with Emma. A pack mule followed on lead.

Ike paused to look back, then ahead.

They moved south once more. Cold increased as they continued south on a cloudy and windy day. Emma, always leading, had fire in her gaze, her mouth tight.

She kept seeing her son Hoag's sweet smile. She remembered the wedding and the pain it caused her, only to be followed by the greatest pain a mother could suffer. Nothing short of Lorena's hanging could give her peace.

On a rise of red cliffs, they reined up in sight of the wide and raging Grand River down below. Red and coursing over the banks, heading for Arizona Territory, the river seemed impossible to cross.

The violent current soared westward. An imposing sight, it promised death to anyone in its path. Even the Ramseys had to dread any effort to cross.

Emma dug in her heels and led the way down to the flat near the flooded north bank.

They all reined up before the ever-rising water.

"Looks bad, Pa," Jonas said. "Maybe we should turn back."

Ike leaned on his pommel and inspected the ground. Rain had washed away any obvious signs, but Ike gestured to his sons to explore.

Jonas rode up the creek to the west, looking for signs.

Harley rode to the east and soon returned.

"Don't see no tracks," Harley said.

Jonas returned, pointing the way he had come. "Some horses headed west."

"Might be a false trail," Ike said. "Corley, you and Crenshaw ride west and see what you come across."

Corley looked annoyed. "You already got men out there, up and down the border."

"Don't argue with me," Ike snapped. "Just have a look, then catch up with us."

Corley hesitated but feared his wrath and nodded.

"Just don't kill the woman," Emma snapped. "She's going to hang."

Ike looked around for signs, turned his horse a couple of times.

"Carson," Ike said as he reined up, "you and Frye head east, just in case they covered their tracks. If you don't find anything, head back to Elk Creek and keep your ears open."

Carson and Frye had no quarrel with going back to civilization, so they headed East without the slightest expression of displeasure.

Corley and Crenshaw turned west, leaving the Ramseys with seven hired guns.

Ike spat and looked around. "Ain't likely they'd try to cross this river no how. And going south to the red desert don't make no sense. They don't call it the badlands for nothing. No sane man would take a woman down there." He paused and spat again. "And maybe that's what they want us to think, so we'll get across and find out."

Jonas frowned. "Pa, it ain't safe. Think of Ma."

But Emma had already dismounted and started an inspection of the trees. Ike and the others dismounted as well.

"Look here!" Emma said, pointing to a tree.

Ike walked over and saw rope burns on the tree bark.

"Pretty fresh," Ike admitted.

Harley came over with an axe from the pack mule. It took hours to build a raft, but meanwhile a rider took ropes across, fighting the harsh current, his big black unwavering. He reached the other side, found signs, and waved toward the south.

Now the task of crossing everyone began.

With the raft secured with ropes, Emma sat on it with the supplies and rode across the rocky current like some kind of warrior queen. Her intent to hang Lorena burned in her gaze. Jealous of Lorena's raving beauty and furious because a woman had not only married her boy but also murdered him, Emma would not rest until this deed was done.

As everyone crossed, a few at a time with the ropes, Emma waited impatiently on the south bank. Ike, ready to camp, found himself overruled by the driven Emma.

"It's hours before dark," she insisted.

Ike had learned to pick his battles with her. He loved her and always would, but she could be really nasty. Whatever happened with the woman, Ike had his own plans for Jeffries.

Leaving the ropes and raft for Corley and Crenshaw, and with Emma in the lead, Ike, Jonas, and Harley followed the tracks of Sam's party, which headed south.

With them rode the seven remaining hired guns led by Rank, a grizzled and nasty man. His second was Rollins—a man with a heavy belly who hated taking orders but could not outdraw Rank—and his backup, the skinny Rums, cut a comic figure when fighting with his big sorrel. The other four born killers were equally smelly and vile.

Night came rather quickly, and even Emma would not ride in the dark.

Riding south the next day, Sam, Hawkins, Lester, Lorena, Asa, and Parker found the going harder: they encountered rough terrain among cliffs, gullies, canyons, and layers of black rock.

Colors of the land, striking with reds and yellows, lay before them. Stray, dark-green junipers and spiny cacti dotted the land under a brilliant-blue sky, even as the rising wind dragged new clouds across the far horizons.

Wind rose and caught a red-tailed hawk in the sky; the bird seemed to stop in midair, surveying the land, looking for a careless prairie dog or any varmint it could eat.

Late in the day, they dismounted to rest their horses in the face of a canyon with high walls and a creek. Sam and Hawkins walked around to look for signs. They found none as the sun moved low in the west.

Sam, not comfortable with moving, noted they had good cover here. "We'll camp over by the creek."

"You're crazy," Parker said. "The army and the San Juan can't be far from here. We're wasting time."

Hawkins shook his head. "Sam's right. In this kind of country, a man rides by instinct."

"Ramsey could be catching up with us," Parker said.

No one disagreed with Parker, but the horses needed rest.

Lorena and Asa, still suffering from their beating, looked exhausted.

Night fell around them as they camped near the creek, deep in the trees where they could hide the horses. Sam had a fire going in a rock pit.

The chill forced them close to the hot fire. They had eaten the fish for breakfast. Now beans, hardtack, and hot coffee gave them warmth but never enough. Asa and Lorena huddled in their blankets toward the heat.

Lester took the first watch and wandered over to the hobbled horses.

Parker sat near Lorena. A greedy and selfish man, he kept hungrily gazing at her. No woman had ever turned him down. His charm had taken him everywhere with every one of them. Yet none had ever got to him until now. He saw Lorena as a goddess and wanted her so deeply that he spent his waking hours planning how it would be with her.

Lorena had no interest in any man just now. Her only need concerned her son. She would do anything to save him and had to stay alive so he would still have a mother who loved him. She had not hesitated to pull the trigger to save Asa, and she would do it again.

Hawkins got up to limp around, his bones feeling the cold.

Asa slept at his mother's side. She gazed at him fondly.

"He's a lucky boy," Parker said, "having you for a mother."

"He worshiped his father," she said.

"Looks like you felt the same."

"Yes, I did."

Sam, uneasy with the conversation, got up and walked down to the busy creek, his gaze scanning the landscape under starry skies crossed with fast-moving clouds.

When he returned, Lorena slept fitfully next to her son.

Sam gazed down at them but didn't sit.

Hawkins huddled in his blankets, drinking more hot coffee.

Parker spoke suddenly. "I'm going to marry that woman."

"She's been through enough," Hawkins said. "Keep away from her."

"Or else," Sam added.

Parker sneered at Sam. "Going soft? I thought you hated women."

Enjoying Sam's dislike of him, which he saw as jealousy, Parker stretched out in his blankets.

"You get the midnight watch," Sam told the gambler.

Parker closed his eyes and slept.

Hawkins downed his coffee and gazed up at the starry sky. Out here in the middle of sand and sage, he felt at home. He rolled in his blankets and fell asleep as soon as he closed his eyes.

Sam paced around, unable to sleep.

From time to time, Sam went to visit Lester and the horses. They both huddled by Lester's little but hot fire. They didn't bother to have a conversation. They had a history and knew each other well. Sam sat by Lester's fire pit to warm his hands.

At midnight and over by the horses, Lester rolled in his blankets near his little fire.

Sam put more chips on Lester's coals, then returned to the main camp. He kicked Parker to wake him and then knelt to build up the main campfire. Sparks flew with the added wood and chips.

Parker grunted, sat up to pour himself some coffee and downed it. Still half asleep, he took his rifle and got up, walking off to stand his watch near the creek.

Lorena and Asa each lay in a deep slumber, close together in their blankets.

Sam, a blanket around him, walked a few feet from the firelight, sat down with his back against a tree and his rifle across his lap and tried to sleep.

Hawkins snored over by the fire. Sam smiled, then sobered.

Out of the firelight, Sam could remember all the times he wanted to forget: bending to give his wife whatever she sought, the ache in his gut when he had to leave the army, the insults she had cast at him when he failed to provide luxury, his hurt pride when she deserted him, and the pain of knowing she and her lover lay dead at the bottom of a cliff.

Yes, he still hated himself, but this ride in the desert took away some of the pain. Gazing up at the sudden stars and moon between the moving clouds, he felt as much at peace as a bitter man could hope to be.

He glanced toward Lorena, a goddess in the eyes of most men. He refused to give an inch in trusting women, yet he felt a need to protect her and her son. He told himself it was chivalry, something any man would do.

Sam heard a sound, a rustle of brush. He sat up straight with his rifle ready. He listened.

Now came a rustle of leaves closer to him.

Parker, beyond the fire and off by the creek, heard nothing and stood oblivious with his rifle in hand. He leaned on the canyon wall, half asleep.

Sam sat waiting, watching, listening.

Now, coming straight for Sam, a small, little, yellow animal with big, dark eyes and floppy ears, its tail limp but wagging.

Realizing it was a pup, Sam set his rifle aside and waited with one hand extended.

The pup whimpered up to Sam's boots. It sniffed the foul leather and looked up, eyes big and round. Its tail wagged with more energy. It sniffed Sam's hand, came even closer. It was a small breed and half grown.

Sam stroked its neck and the back of its left ear.

He spoke softly. "Hey, little fellah."

In the moonlight, Sam read the collar on the pup's neck: US ARMY.

Sam took a chunk of jerky from his pocket. The pup crawled onto his knee, then his thigh, grabbing the hard meat and settling against Sam's gun belt as it chewed.

When the pup had stopped eating, Sam took it up in his arms and got to his feet.

The pup snuggled against him as he carried it around the campfire.

He knelt by Asa, who slept close to Lorena, also deep in slumber. Sam put the pup down on Asa's chest and drew the blanket partly over it.

The little dog lay quiet on Asa's heartbeat.

When the pup licked Asa's face, the boy awakened, startled.

Seeing the pup snuggling with him, Asa had a happy grin on his face. Asa held the dog against him and looked up at Sam with a smile to treasure. Then the boy closed his eyes, and both he and the pup fell sound asleep.

Sam turned away. He wiped at his eyes.

⊰⊱

Daybreak cast long shadows across Sam's camp in the mouth of a canyon near a creek.

Lorena awakened to yawn and sat up, startled to see the dog in her sleeping son's arms. They looked so peaceful, she finally smiled. She looked over at Parker asleep in his bedroll, at Hawkins shaking the coffee pot, and Sam off by the creek. She saw Lester over by the horses as he led them into the canyon.

She smiled again at Asa and the pup.

She stood up, suddenly startled for the second time. Far to the south and across the open land and hard against the southern horizon, a dense black cloud seemed to be moving toward them.

She came over to Hawkins and knelt for coffee. "Mr. Hawkins, look."

He followed her gaze to the black threat. "I seen it."

They both stood up as Sam came over to them.

"May pass us by," Sam said, "but just the same, we'll pack up and get into the canyon, as high above the creek as we can."

A rising wind suddenly blew sand and dust around them.

Lorena's hair whipped about her face. She went to awaken Asa and his pup.

The wind took Hawkins's hat, but he quickly grabbed it.

The fury of the approaching black cloud stretched miles wide.

Hawkins kicked sand over the fire, then booted Parker awake.

The wind grabbed Asa and the pup. Sam swept them up, blankets and all, and carried them toward the canyon.

Parker stumbled to his feet but fell flat on his face in the wind.

Hawkins grabbed Lorena's hand, yanking her along.

"Put a blanket over your face," Hawkins yelled.

Lorena used her free hand to do as he bid.

Parker got up again and fell down again, the wind tossing him back.

Sand and dust whipped everything with savage fury.

Inside the canyon, Sam's party sought shelter against the south wall, as far back and as high as they could get. Scrub brush and boulders offered some protection.

Sam took ropes and bound Asa and Lorena, both wrapped in a blanket, to a stump of a juniper. He hovered over them, tying himself against them. As Sam lay across them, his face near Lorena's, he pulled another blanket over them.

Lester and Hawkins kept the horses tied and hobbled as far back as they could get and still have shelter behind rocks. The two men doubled up, wrapping blankets around themselves.

Parker looked numb, never having been in such a spot, and continued to stumble for cover.

Wind howled into the canyon. Dust, pebbles, and limbs flew in the air.

Their world went from sunlight to dark.

And now they could see it, the side-winding twister touching down with vengeance some distance away from the mouth of the canyon. Its roar was thunderous, and it continued north, away from them, but its wrath reached far and wide.

Hail suddenly pounded them like driven nails.

The twister sounded like a locomotive.

The black cloud of death crossed over them with raging fury. The funnel disappeared north in the cloud, leaving heavy hail. Yet no one in the canyon dared to move, not until the roar of the funnel abated.

Sam's face brushed up against Lorena's, then Asa's. Lorena welcomed Sam's strong arms around them, while he felt the soft warmth of her. They all had their eyes shut tight, until the hail suddenly stopped and the darkness gave way to sudden sunlight.

Asa, grateful for Sam's protection, hugged his pup.

The sun, so bright it blinded them, became warm and friendly.

◄►

To the north as the storm raged, Ike Ramsey, Emma, Jonas, and Harley, along with their seven men, sought shelter in the depth of the high ridges.

"I seen one of 'em take a whole herd of cattle," Ike yelled over the roar.

Hail pounded them as blackness came like a blanket.

The twister raced past the ridges and spun and leaped to the sky and disappeared in the clouds. Flooding rain swept the Ramseys and their horses while they waited for it to pass.

The sun spread new light as the storm moved north.

Undeterred, Emma stood strong and ready to move.

Chapter 4

Sam's party was still taking shelter in the canyon. The twister had passed with the black storm, leaving them in bright sunlight but drenched.

Sam freed himself, along with Lorena and her son, who still held the pup.

Lester and Hawkins brought forward the still-frantic horses. Hawkins went out to check the camp, then returned to the canyon. Parker, deeply frightened by the twister, tried to appear calm and composed.

"Camp is plumb gone," Hawkins said.

Lorena sat on a rock with her son and the pup. Asa's eyes remained wide with the trauma.

"We got to move on," Parker said.

Hawkins growled at him. "You ain't running this outfit, Parker."

Parker glared at him and then at Sam, who was brushing off his buckskin.

Fearing a flash flood from the cliffs, they remade camp on higher ground, just outside the canyon, and built a fire with brush and chips that were wet and smoking.

Lorena moved closer to Sam and his buckskin. She nodded at the pup as Asa played with it near the fire.

"It has an army collar," she said softly. "What does it mean?"

"Nothing yet."

"There will be an army camp?"

"That's what we were told."

Lorena felt no confidence from his response and turned away.

On the next morning, Sam's party rode south toward crimson bluffs, beyond which lay the San Juan River. Lester brought along the two packhorses in the rear while Hawkins scouted ahead.

Later, Sam, Lorena, Parker, and Asa, with the pup on his lap, reined up as Hawkins came riding back toward them. Hawkins drew up to Sam.

"I found the army camp. They pretty much pulled up their stakes weeks ago." He grimaced. "Seems like they left a squad in charge. Four dead, shot in the back. Old arrows stuck in them to frame Apaches. Pockets and gear picked clean. Horses run off."

They waited for Hawkins to draw a deep breath and continue.

"Five of 'em skedaddled on shod horses. Ain't no signs on either side of the river. All washed out. But deserters for sure."

Sam frowned. "Can we ford the San Juan?"

"Yeah," Hawkins said. "It's up, but it ain't deep, so we'll make it."

Parker mumbled to himself.

Lorena and Asa looked to Sam for leadership.

They all knew danger could be over the next bluff.

Sam and Hawkins rode far ahead of the others.

※

At twilight under clear skies, Sam's party reached the bluff overlooking the wide and racing San Juan River—which thankfully was shallow. The army camp, to the east, was not in view.

They made their way down to the river and easily rode across to the south side as night fell around them. Sam wanted the San Juan between them and the Ramseys, should they appear suddenly.

They made camp with no view of the army post over on the north side.

After situating Lorena and her son by a hot campfire with Parker on guard, Sam, Hawkins, and Lester rode back across the river and made their way to the looted remains of the army post.

The dead soldiers, whom Lester partially covered with blankets, still had arrows protruding. Sam walked around a few minutes, viewing the disaster in the bright moonlight.

"Hawkins, you're right," Sam said. "A platoon pulled out weeks ago and headed east."

After collecting identification but finding the dead had been looted of all else, the three men rode back across the river. Lester took the horses while Hawkins and Sam came back to the fire to report.

"Now what?" Parker asked.

"We'll bury 'em first light," Sam said. "And keep riding south."

"There's shelter at some old ruins south of here," Hawkins said. "We could be there tomorrow night."

Parker, ever the doomsayer, grunted. "Yeah, and where are those deserters?—they're probably just waiting for us"

"Don't you worry, sonny," Hawkins said, "I'll protect you."

Parker smirked. "You couldn't protect yourself. You're just an old man."

"Come on, try me," Hawkins said.

"Parker, back off," Sam snapped. "I'm real tired of you."

Parker, weary and afraid of what lay ahead, did not argue.

Everyone, exhausted and tired, made little conversation while they had coffee, hardtack, and beans before calling it a night. Sam took the first watch.

⋈

Back north on the prairie, the Ramseys and their seven hired guns made camp on the same night.

"We ain't never gonna catch 'em," Harley complained.

"The horses are still rattled from the lightning," Jonas said.

"Stop your bellyaching," Ike growled.

Emma stood beyond the firelight, gazing south.

Lorena had been too pretty for Emma's taste, and Emma felt the constant irritation of Hoag having slept with that Kansas woman, only to be brutally murdered. To Emma, Hoag could do no wrong, and the pain of his loss would be burning in her until that woman was dead.

Neither her husband nor sons ventured near her.

Down at the creek with the horses, Harley and Jonas shivered as they kept the horses quiet.

Jonas spoke in a low voice. "Harley, we got to stop this."

"Stop what?"

"We can't let Ma hang that poor woman."

Jonas fretted as he stroked a horse's mane.

Harley softened. "Listen, kid, to start with, we may never find 'em. And remember that Pa's got nothing on his mind but getting Jeffries for killing Uncle Joe. So there'll be one devil of a fight. Nobody knows how that'll come out. We could all be dead when it's over. So just lie back and wait to see what happens."

Jonas finally agreed in silence as they walked back to the firelight. Their mother sat by the fire with nothing to say.

Harley rolled up in his blankets and began to snore.

Jonas, restless, drew a blanket around him and walked into the night to where he could look up at the stars. Shortly thereafter, his mother suddenly appeared at his side. She also had a blanket around her.

"Jonas, are you all right?"

Jonas got brave. "Do you have family back in Cheyenne?"

Her sudden anger faded. "No, there's no one. Our family is right here."

Jonas drew the blanket tight around him as chills ran through him. He wanted to tell her he had seen the raid on the Madison spread, watching from the ridge. He knew about their other raids and how some of the hired guns had ravaged the women. He didn't want any more of it.

"Ma, let's turn back. What we're doing, it's wrong."

"You're a good boy, Jonas. And that's really too bad."

She hesitated a long moment, then turned and walked back to the campfire.

Jonas gazed off into the night. She had never paid much attention to him with Hoag around. He had not minded it much, as he preferred to be on his own, so it didn't matter, even now. Nothing, not even what might be in Cheyenne, mattered—except that he had to save Lorena and the boy.

⬥⬥⬥

At daybreak, the soldiers were buried near the abandoned camp and away from the north bank of the San Juan River.

White, bare bluffs behind them, Sam and his party continued south from the river. Hawkins took the lead, scouting ahead through high, grassy hills. They rode through scattered sage with a pungent smell and swarming with hungry insects.

Sam rode his buckskin ahead of Parker, Lorena, and Asa, followed by Lester with the two packhorses.

Sam tried not to think of the violent storm that forced him so close to Lorena and the boy, but he could still feel her face against his when he had held them safe. He had seen nothing but sweetness in her, and he hated Hoag for having been anywhere near her. Truly beautiful, she had suffered enough, and Sam would protect her to the death. Then, he told himself, he would just ride away.

Sam tried to concentrate on the cloudy sky, the restless prairie, and the crimson ridges crossed with yellow in the east. Beyond the ridges rose dark, forested mountains.

They all rode in silence for most of the day.

Hawkins rode back to Sam's side and gestured east across the prairie toward distant riders. Sam halted their trek to take out his spyglass.

"Five of 'em. One's a sergeant," Sam said. "It's them, all right."

"Keeping pace with us," Hawkins said.

"How far to the ruins?"

"Be there by nightfall."

"They see us, all right," Sam said, lowering the glass.

"And the woman."

Sam nodded, grim and disturbed.

Hawkins rode on ahead. Sam started to ride, the others behind him.

Prickly pear cacti were everywhere and ready to bloom.

As they rode through sage, a black-tailed rabbit leaped into the air and sped away into the brush. Overhead, a red-tailed hawk sailed along but lost sight of the rabbit.

As Sam and his party moved south, they were closer to the ridges and to the deserters. Soon, all in the party could see the five men, and Parker looked real nervous. He rode up along Lorena's left side; her son was on her right.

"Not good," Parker said to Lorena. "Those men have nothing to lose."

"I'm paying all of you to keep us safe," she reminded him.

"We may not live to be paid," Parker said. "Maybe an advance will help."

"You'll be paid in Texas."

Parker realized he had crossed the line from romance to avarice and had to make amends. "Just making conversation."

Lorena did not respond, but Asa looked at Parker as if he wanted to hit him.

Asa cuddled the pup but remained angry.

Parker rode on ahead to keep the peace. He caught up with Sam.

"You think those deserters will come after us?"

Sam nodded. "Tonight."

Parker fell back in silence, knowing Sam disliked him intensely.

Sam looked to the east and the deserters, who were keeping ace with them.

As twilight came, Hawkins came riding back.

"I see the ruins," Hawkins told Sam.

As night fell and the stars twinkled in the moving clouds above, Sam and his party came to the ruins, another rancho that had been deserted long ago, probably because of Indian raids. This one had no roof, only broken walls.

The prairie spread low and sinister around them. The moon rose slowly but hid behind the clouds and gave little light.

Hawkins rode about and reported to Sam. "No one's been around for some time."

They made camp inside the adobe walls. The outside walls were a foot thick but down to four- to five-feet high, while most of the inside walls had crumbled to the ground. Just outside the north wall, an old well with a wooden bucket provided cool water for the horses and for everyone's canteens.

The old stone chimney and hearth, without any roof, stood in the largest room and was used for a fire. Coffee and beans steamed in the hearth to warm them through the night.

The horses were tethered inside the north wall.

Lorena and Asa huddled near the hot flames of smelly chips and brush. Hawkins came from the north wall for coffee and gave them another blanket.

"Why would anyone live out here?" she asked.

"Folks want their own place," Hawkins said, refilling his coffee cup. "But either Injuns or bad weather run 'em off."

"It's so lonely," she said.

"Wait till you see the badlands. After we cross the mountains, it ain't nothing God intended."

There was no sign of the deserters, but everyone knew that would not last.

"Won't those men just keep riding south to get away?" Lorena asked.

Hawkins downed his coffee and shook his head. "When a man deserts, he gets real mean. And hungry, and they know we got you with us."

Parker cast a nasty look at Hawkins and took up his rifle. "This is one devil of an outfit. A fired lawman, an old fool, and an old, crippled-up man."

Hawkins grunted. "And a big-mouthed card sharp."

Hawkins pulled a blanket around him, took his rifle, and returned to the north wall.

Parker paced around nervously, glaring at Sam. "We should go back."

Sam looked around the ruins in the dark of night. "Parker, you take the south side. Hawkins has the north side with the horses. Lester, you keep an eye on the west. I'll take the east wall."

"And when do we sleep?" Parker demanded.

Sam grimaced. "They're cold and hungry out there, and they ain't waiting. Just get ready."

Parker took his blanket and rifle, then sneered and walked over to the nearly four-foot-high south wall, settling down near an open crack but under good cover, where he planned to stay. Hawkins remained behind the north wall while Lester huddled by the west side, each of them with blankets but some fifty feet from the chimney and its fire.

Lorena and Asa huddled in blankets by the struggling flames in the hearth. Asa slept close to her with his pup at his side.

Sam, away from the fire and by the east wall, which barely rose three feet, watched the night with piercing eyes. He felt the cold, the tension, and the responsibility, all of which grew heavier by the hour. He could never let anything happen to Lorena and her son.

At the fireside, Lorena smiled as Lester, a blanket around him and a rifle in hand, came to kneel. She poured him hot coffee.

"Lester, aren't you cold?" she asked.

"No, ma'am, I ain't been cold since the Comanches got me."

"I'm sorry."

"Everyone says it made me crazy. Am I crazy, ma'am?"

"No, Lester, just experienced."

Lester grinned. "Yes, ma'am, real experienced."

Lester looked happy. He took his cup with him and hurried back to the west wall.

⌐⌐

Later that night at the ruins, pale light came from an elusive moon often hiding behind the dark, moving clouds. The silent prairie spread for miles in all directions.

A hungry coyote moved through the sage in sight of the ruins, then wandered off into the night. Lizards with big eyes checked out the walls but hid from view.

Lorena, wrapped in her blankets, lay near the fire. Her glorious hair glistened like gold in the firelight. She gazed into the flames, saw the kind, rugged face of her first husband as he held Asa on his shoulder, the vicious snarl on Hoag's face as he attacked her son, and then the grimness of Sam's narrowed gaze. A tear ran down her cheek.

Long after midnight, Lorena slept alone facing the fire. No sign of Asa or the pup. Moonlight struggled to shine through the drifting clouds.

Nearby, sleeping men appeared to be in bedrolls with hats on the upper ends of the saddles.

A hush fell over the night. Not even a lone coyote broke the stillness.

Suddenly, five deserters appeared in the pale light. They came through the missing doorway at the east side and stopped to see the firelight shining on Lorena's golden hair.

A burly former sergeant with a crooked nose, his stripes half torn from his sleeve, a six-gun in hand, leered at the sleeping beauty and the sleeping men in their blankets. He gazed at Lorena with lust and smacked his lips.

A grizzly corporal with a nervous twitch at his mouth and a ready six-gun came up beside him. They both had a good look at her hair and saw a glimpse of her face and the rose of her left cheek.

Three privates with wild eyes and grizzled faces held back but kept their rifles aimed. At the sergeant's wave, they fired into the bedrolls, which shuddered from the impact. Their shots echoed in the night.

Lorena sat up, frightened, and turned to stare up at the intruders. The blanket fell back from her feminine shape, revealing a tear on her dress at the sleeve. She glanced at the shot-up bodies and put her hand over her mouth to stop her scream.

The former sergeant sneered. "Don't you worry ma'am. We got better plans for you."

As the privates held back, the sergeant and corporal moved toward her.

Sam's voice rang out behind the wall near the five deserters.

"Drop 'em! Now!"

The deserters, with nothing to lose, spun but couldn't see him, so they started to fire at the shadows.

Sam, Hawkins, and Lester fired from cover of the east and west walls.

The deserters were hit hard; they spun and fell.

Lorena leaped up to avoid the sergeant's body.

With the attackers fallen, Parker made a belated appearance. Asa appeared with the pup in his arms. Sam, Hawkins, and Lester moved from cover.

The sergeant, still alive but on his side, tried to rise with a gun in hand. Sam kicked the weapon from his hand. Blood all over him, the sergeant lay back, staring up at Sam.

Sam glared down at him.

"Why'd you kill your own men?" Sam asked.

The sergeant choked on his words, the syllables jamming in his throat. He saw the pup and smiled before he closed his eyes and jerked straight. The sergeant was dead.

Lorena, still shaken, shivered as she drew her blanket tight. Parker came and put an arm around her.

"You're a brave woman," Parker said, "for acting as bait."

"Where were you?" she asked.

"Right behind the others."

"Yeah," Hawkins said, "way behind."

Parker glared at him. Lorena moved away to be on her own. Parker turned nervously and walked the perimeter, pretending to be on guard.

Hawkins, hit on the left arm, sat by the fire. Lorena hurried to help him. She fussed over his wound and wrapped it. Asa, holding his pup, sat by Hawkins and watched.

Sam, pouring coffee, grinned at Hawkins. "You did all right."

"For an old cripple? Maybe I get a hitch in my get-along when it's cold, but I can still whip you, sonny."

Sam handed him the cup as Lorena finished bandaging the old man's left arm.

Lester brought up the deserters' horses. He dumped money from the sergeant's saddlebags.

"Must have been over the payroll," Sam said. "Check their boots before you bury 'em."

Parker, drawn by the sight of the money, wet his lips.

Sam ignored the gambler as he re-stuffed the saddlebags. "We'll turn it over to the army or the law, whichever comes first."

Sam gazed toward the deserters' worn-out horses as Lester turned them loose, unsaddled. Sam hated seeing horses mistreated.

At daybreak at the ruins, the horses were saddled, and the two packhorses were loaded.

Chill remained from the night. No wind. Dark clouds were moving in from the far south, encroaching on the blue sky. Lorena, Parker, and Asa stood together.

Sam looked east at the rugged mountains with the spyglass.

Hawkins and Lester came over to follow his gaze.

"You been up there?" Sam asked them.

Hawkins nodded. "Pretty rugged. A big creek runs through, but you can't stay with it the whole way. You're up and down them ridges trying to follow it. On the far end, there's a long, narrow canyon to get out in the open and right into the Badlands. Better carry enough water. But it's not far from there to Little River."

Sam considered it. "If it's a short cut, we may have a chance to beat the Ramseys to Texas."

"You're assuming," Hawkins said, "that they didn't go east on the San Juan and down into New Mexico Territory."

"Ike Ramsey's smarter than that," Sam said. "He's as good a tracker as we are. He also likes an easy trail. He may avoid the mountains and head south on the army road and try to cut us off on the other side."

Hawkins gazed toward the mountains. "Them mountains can be for us or against us."

They all mounted and rode east toward the mountains.

Sam led the way on his big buckskin, leaning down often to stroke its neck.

Chapter 5

Late the next day, coming from the north with Emma riding in the lead, the Ramsey party came to the same ruins where Sam's party had camped and fought the deserters.

Emma had a fury in her face and a gleam in her eyes that had not lessened.

Ike wanted to hang Sam for having killed Ike's brother, but hanging a woman, especially a beautiful one, was Emma's idea, not his. But everyone, including Ike, was afraid of her.

Rums had problems with his ornery, tall, long-legged sorrel as they came onto the abandoned site. Five new graves were nearby. Ike dismounted to read signs.

"Some kind of fight," Ike said, "maybe cut them down in size."

"Maybe it had something to do with those lame horses we saw," Harley said.

Ike made a face. "But something's funny here. They headed east toward the mountains."

Ike knelt, studied the dirt, and stood again as darkness fell around them.

"They're scared," Rank suggested.

Ike shook his head. "Jeffries is trying to cut across. It'll take 'em a lot longer than our going south on the army road. And he can't get around the badlands. Maybe he ain't smart enough to figure that out."

"Rank's got it right. They're running scared," Harley said.

"Jeffries ain't afraid of nothing," Ike warned, "and you'd best remember that. He's a man looking to die, and he don't much care how."

"So now what?" Harley asked.

"Tomorrow, me and you and Jonas will ride south. With Emma."

Ike turned to Rank, gestured toward the mountains.

"Rank, come daylight, you and the boys keep on their trail but not too close. We'll head 'em off when they come out the other side."

Rums dismounted. As he moved to unsaddle, the sorrel bit at him. Rums punched it on the jaw. It bit at him again. The other hired guns just laughed.

⊣⊢

At nightfall, Sam's party rested inside the foothills, where they found good cover.

They made camp near a little, singing creek. They chanced a fire in a hole surrounded by rocks. Lorena took Asa, along with his pup, for a walk along the creek.

Lester tended the horses nearby. Hawkins stood guard on higher ground.

Sam and Parker paused to watch Lorena and her son from a distance. Moonlight glistened on her yellow hair.

"She favors me," Parker said.

"Leave her alone."

"I'm a gentleman." He looked Sam over. "You're just not in her class."

Parker turned and started to follow Lorena.

Sam tripped him. Parker crashed against a rock and turned, still upright.

"I said stay away from her," Sam growled.

"Haven't you ruined enough women?"

Furious, Sam stepped forward. The two men rushed each other. They grappled and rolled, fighting furiously. They pounded each other, locked arms, kicked, and grunted. Parker's hat went flying.

At the creek, Lorena and Asa turned to stare.

Sam and Parker rolled in the dirt, squirming to get at each other. They pounded and hit. Breaking, they scrambled to their feet, facing each other some ten feet apart.

Lorena, Asa at her heels, came hurrying back to the camp.

"Stop it," she said.

Parker gasped for breath. "We're just fighting over you, ma'am."

She glared at them. "I said stop it or you won't get paid."

The two men broke their stances. Sam wiped his face with the back of his hand.

Parker, breathing hard, picked up his hat and turned to her.

"Where are you keeping the money?" Parker asked her. "In that purse? Your stockings?"

Her chin went up in anger.

Parker backed off. "Ma'am, I'm sorry. It's Jeffries's fault. He's trying my patience."

"And you're both trying mine," she said.

Lorena sat by the fire in the pit, her back to them. Asa sat near her.

Sam walked away, gazing into the night.

⚜

Late that night in Sam's camp.

Sam gazed at Lorena and her son as they slept near the fire pit. The little dog was nestled next to Asa.

Parker also slept. Hawkins and Lester were still out on guard.

Sam walked through the trees to the creek where it skipped along but had run over from time to time. A large pool had formed on one side by the trees.

Sam, alone by the pool in the moonlight, knelt and listened to the silence of the night. An unhappy man, he still loved the smell of the pines and some sweet-smelling flowers he could not see.

He was a big, tough man who could outshoot, outfight, and outride most of the west, but that one thorn in his side, left by his wife, still lingered.

In some ways, he knew, Ike Ramsey suffered the same problem with Emma. Sam had witnessed it, and he had understood how a woman could get under a man's skin. It had to be Ike's only weakness.

Sam tried to be philosophical, to roll with it, to look only ahead.

He sensed someone approaching. He stood up, putting a hand on his gun belt, only to see Asa walking toward him in the moonlight. Asa's little dog nipped at his heels.

Sam didn't ask why the boy wandered about in the night. He understood and sat back down at the water's edge, gazing at the slight ripples in the pale light.

Asa came to sit beside him. Silent, the boy moved a bit closer. The dog ran around them as it played. Sam, comfortable with the boy at his side, picked up a flat rock.

"Can you do this?" Sam asked.

Sam skipped it across the water. It seemed to dance on the ripples until it hit the far bank.

Asa grinned. He picked up a little rock and tried to skip it, but it just went ker plunk.

Sam found another flat rock. He took Asa's hand and helped him throw the rock.

The rock skipped. Asa looked up with a big grin.

Sam grinned back. They tossed some more rocks. Sam had never had a son, for which he had once prayed, and this boy temporarily filled a spot in Sam's heart.

Asa sat close to him and gazed across the pool, then up at the moon and stars. He smiled with the chill of night, the beauty of the mountains, and this big man at his side. They listened to chirps and whistles in the darkness and now the faraway howl of a lone coyote.

They sat in silence, side by side. The pup chewed on Asa's boot.

Back at camp, Lorena, having awakened and missing Asa, wrapped a blanket about herself and walked into the moonlight. She saw Sam and her son seated by the dark pool. She walked down to them but stopped to listen as Sam followed Asa's gaze to the stars.

"Up in Montana country," Sam said, "the stars are so close you can almost reach up and grab one."

An excited Asa scooped up water in his hands, tossed it up, and clapped.

Sam nodded. "No, I haven't seen the geysers or the boiling pots, but Hawkins has."

Asa, enthralled, pointed to a tall aspen.

Sam understood. "Yes, big timber up there, and the lodgepole pines near reach the sky. But out in California, they got redwood trees so tall you feel like if you climb one, you can shake God's hand."

Lorena, touched, stood back and listened.

Asa smiled as he gazed up at Sam, who had little experience talking with youngsters and had difficulty coming up with more excitement.

"You ever see buffalo?" Sam asked.

Asa shook his head, waiting.

"Old timers say that in the early years, the herds were so big, it took three days for 'em to pass," Sam said. "They made real thunder when they started running. Nothing left alive after that."

Asa spread his arms wide in question.

"Yes, it's big country up there," Sam said, "but not as big as Texas, where you can get lost and never find your way back."

Asa straightened, expecting more. Sam picked up another rock and sent it skipping across the water. Turning, Sam felt relieved to see Lorena walking over to them.

"Asa, you need your sleep," she said.

The boy stood reluctantly. Asa looked down at Sam and suddenly leaned over to hug Sam around the neck and shoulder. The hug lasted so long that Sam could only hold his breath in gratitude. Asa then jumped up and left with his pup at his heels.

Sam and Lorena were alone. It made him nervous.

She knelt near where he sat. "He's never done that before."

Sam did not respond. He sent a rock skimming across the water.

"I thank you for being so nice to Asa," she said. "You see, when he was only five, his father was killed when their wagon overturned in a storm. He was pinned with him under the wagon all night. He nearly died from exposure, and he hasn't spoken a word since."

Sam picked up a rock and skipped it across the shining water.

"Doctors think it may take something just as bad to bring him back."

Sam liked having her near and wanted to show off, despite himself. She watched Sam skim another rock. She picked up a rock, tried to skip it. It fell into the water.

"How do you do that?" she asked.

Sam picked up another rock and demonstrated how to skip it across the water.

Lorena tried again. The rock fell flat. Sam picked up a little flat rock and handed it to her and showed her how to flick her wrist.

She tried again. The rock danced across the water. Delighted, she clapped her hands together. A smile crossed her face but only for a moment.

She sat back and wrapped her blanket more closely about her.

Sitting quietly and listening to the night sounds, they had sudden and difficult thoughts.

Lorena, having lost a good man many years ago, then having shot the drunken Hoag, had a dim view of what kind of world awaited her and her son. If they could escape Emma's lynch mob and reach her stoic brothers in Texas, they'd be safe. But then Sam would disappear from their lives, and right now she sat wrapped in the nearness of this big, strong, powerful man. In fact, she wished with all her heart that he'd put his arm around her and protect her.

Sitting next to Lorena, he knew her very touch would be more than he could bear. Never had he met a woman so beautiful and brave yet so vulnerable and so devoted her to son. He wanted to put his arm around her, but he couldn't move. When she spoke out of the silence, he felt his heart jump.

"I've done a terrible thing to you," she said. "The Ramseys are going to murder all of us."

"They may just let you go."

"Not Emma. You see, as Hoag's widow, my name will go on the deed, and after me, Asa's, so she can't let us live."

Sam swallowed hard, understanding Lorena's plight more fully, and even though he knew she couldn't profit if it was murder, he knew full well it had been self-defense and excusable homicide when protecting the life of her son. If it came to that, a court would order her name on the deed. Emma had to know that as well.

Just as Lorena said, Emma would never let her or the boy walk away from this fight.

He stared across the pond. She got to her feet and paused, but he did not move or look up. She lifted her skirts above the dirt and turned back to camp.

Sam slowly stood. He worried about her and the boy. He worried about himself for the feelings being stirred inside of him by her very presence, feelings buried so long ago.

⚬⚬

At Ike's camp at the ruins and early in the morning, only Ike, Emma, and their two sons were still in camp.

Jonas and Harley were sitting cross-legged by the campfire, stuffing themselves with bacon and beans, while Emma fussed over them like a mother hen.

The seven hired guns rode toward the mountains with Rank in the lead. Ike, at the east adobe wall, watched them become just a spot in the distance as they neared the mountains. Sam's party had to be at least two days ahead of them.

Ike, a cup of coffee in hand, turned to see two riders approach from the north.

Corley and Crenshaw finally rode into camp and dismounted. They loosened cinches, then headed for the fire to enjoy the hot coffee.

Corley squatted with his coffee. Crenshaw stretched and remained standing.

Ike watched the tiny blur of the hired guns disappear into the mountains. He downed his coffee and then came over to the campfire.

"We didn't have to go far," Corley said. "Ran into some of our boys. Seems four fellas was just riding back to Elk Creek. And there weren't no woman with 'em. It was just a trick, that's all."

Emma glared east at the mountains. Somewhere in that rugged range rode a woman who had claim to a share of the Ramseys' giant spread. Her claim on the deed had no chance of removal without lengthy litigation, which Emma knew would end in Lorena's favor. There remained only one way to remove Lorena's threat forever.

Emma kept her eye on Jonas. Somehow, she had to keep him out of the way. Knowing Jonas's aversion to violence, it might not be too hard.

⁂

At daybreak, Sam and his party were riding east through the mountains.

Sam led. Hawkins, Parker, Lorena, and Asa with his pup followed in single file on a high wall overlooking a rocky canyon to their left. Lester followed with the two packhorses.

Sam would glance back often to be sure Lorena and her son could handle the ride. He saw only determination and grit. He admired them both. He felt weary, but he knew they had to be even more worn down.

Parker turned in the saddle to look around and tipped his hat to Lorena, who rode behind him. She nodded, but her hands, tightly clenching the reins, reflected her fear and how weary she was. Asa, behind her, rode in silence with his frisky pup in his arms.

Rocks were everywhere in this mean country. No longer in the hot desert sun, they felt the cold of the mountains cut right to their bones.

The horses often stumbled and fought the bit. Their sweat sent up steam.

Lorena, tired and pale, her hair falling about her face, managed to keep up.

Asa watched her and worried.

Rocks and chunks of earth rolled from their horses' hooves.

Late in the day, Sam and his party reined up in the trees on the ridge. The trail dropped hundreds of feet down to their left, but on their right, they found high ground, many springs, and plenty of trees for cover.

Sam peered back along the ridge using his spyglass and saw no one at first. Then he could barely make out the seven men on the prairie, so far back they were just dots in the open. Sam felt certain the trees hid his own party from their view.

Parker, grumbling, snapped at Sam. "We oughta rest."

"Can't," Sam said. The others turned to follow Sam's gaze.

"Ramsey?" Hawkins asked.

Lorena put her hand over her mouth to muffle a cry.

"How far back?" Hawkins persisted.

Sam turned. "Two days or less. Seven riders. Can't make 'em out. But they can't see us in these trees. We got to follow the ridge and stay under cover until we find a way down. But no talking and no gunfire. Walk your horses. And keep 'em quiet."

Sam and his party dismounted. They quietly led their horses along the ridge, the trees and boulders covering them well.

                                                             ✥

On the trail heading toward the mountains, the Ramseys' seven hired guns, led by Rank, rode the open prairie. These ugly, nasty men had no interest in anyone except themselves, and they always spent what Ike Ramsey paid them within one trip to town. Except this time, they were receiving double pay.

Later in the day, aware that Sam's trail led onto the high ridge, they came to a halt.

Rollins looked around. "I don't like this. We could be riding into a trap."

Rank stretched. "Want to go back?"

"You're kidding, right? Ever see what the Ramseys do to anybody what crosses 'em?"

Rums's sorrel twisted its head back and bit at Rums's boot. Rums growled at the animal. "Blast you—just wait. When we get outta these mountains, I'm gonna beat the devil out of you."

The other men just laughed, but Rank couldn't let it alone.

"Hey, Rums, you figured what's wrong with that horse of yours? He don't know he's a gelding. He thinks it never happened."

Again, more laughter.

As they sobered, Rank looked up toward the right to the ridge trail. They might catch them somewhere down the line. They knew their prey would head east, one way or another.

⚔

All parties were on the move.

Sam, Hawkins, Parker, Lester, Lorena, and Asa with his pup trailing, walked in heavy woods on the ridge, leading their horses. Lester also led the two packhorses, one of which now had a light load due to the journey.

A far distance behind, the Ramseys' seven hired guns, though unable to see Sam's party, followed their prey's trail on horseback.

Back in the desert and heading south to skirt the mountains, Ike, Emma, Jonas, Harley, Corley, and Crenshaw rode with Emma in the lead.

⚔

The night was black around the seven hired guns, so they stopped on the narrow ridge trail. The going had worn them down with the rocks, brambles, and the dangerous edge and frightening drop to their left.

They caught no sign of Sam's party, only the occasional tracks in the trees.

"We'll camp here," Rank said. "And be quiet. No fire."

⚔

Later that night at Sam's camp on the ridge, they kept no fire. The temperature became colder by the minute.

Lorena huddled, wrapped in blankets with her son. Both shivered. The dog lay on top of them, chewing on a blanket's edge. Against a boulder, they lay nestled in a circle of rocks. Lester stood guard on a rise.

Sam, standing near the horses, checked the load in his Winchester. Hawkins stood near him. They worried for Lorena and her son, not for the men, who could take care of themselves.

Parker walked around nervously. He had misgivings about whether this venture would be worth all this hardship and irritation. Yet when he saw Lorena's golden hair gleaming in the moonlight as she slept with her son, he felt that same driving need for her.

Sam and Hawkins looked at the shivering Lorena and Asa.

Hawkins shook his head. "Got to take a chance on a fire, get some warm food in 'em, or they ain't gonna make it."

"You're right," Sam grunted.

"Besides, ain't no hiding our trail up here."

Parker came over to glare at Sam. "I told you, we should have gone south and around. You got no business leading this party. I'm going to let her choose who's actually in charge."

"Keep your voice down," Sam snapped.

Sam broke off some of the brush and stomped it with his boot.

Off the ridge trail, Sam knelt to dig a fire pit with his knife. Hawkins helped pile rocks around it as Sam got the sticks burning.

Hawkins then went to escort Lorena and her son, along with his pup, over to sleep by the warm flames. She sat up in her blankets, next to her son and his pup.

Parker came to kneel at her side. "How about it, ma'am? I'm educated and a gentleman. I've been in the army. I was an officer. I should be in charge."

Lorena looked from him to Sam but remained silent.

Parker persisted. "Jeffries can't be trusted. Look at the fix we're in."

Sam shoved more crushed brush into the pit of crackling flames.

An annoyed Parker continued. "Like I said, ma'am, I should be in charge. And since it's your money, I'm asking you to agree."

Lorena hugged her son. She looked away.

Sam got up and, with Hawkins, gathered more limbs and chunks of rotten wood. They piled it near the fire. Then Hawkins put more wood in the flames.

Parker was not giving up. "Ma'am?"

She shook her head, snuggled down with her son as close to the fire as was safe.

Parker, agitated, stood up and folded his arms in the cold.

"Just remember, ma'am, I won't be responsible for anything that happens."

Farther back on the ridge, the seven hired guns suffered through their cold camp and could not see Sam's fire, not even a glow. They shivered in the dark, afraid to alert Sam of their proximity; they were unaware that they had been spotted already.

Later that night at Sam's camp, the fire burned hot in the crevice close to where Lorena, her son, and his pup were sleeping. Sam sat watching them, his coffee cup in his hands.

Lester slept with his habitual smile on his face. Hawkins lay sleeping with his back to the fire. Parker stood guard away from the camp, out of earshot.

Lorena sat up, wrapped in her blankets, and warmed her hands over the fire. Sam filled a cup with hot coffee and handed it to her. She took it in both hands, the cup warming her fingers. She spoke in a low voice without meeting his gaze.

"Are you crazy, Mr. Jeffries?"

"Most likely."

"Maybe it's the land."

Sam shook his head in silence.

"Then it's being so far from civilization. From convention."

Parker, rifle in hand, abruptly came back to the fire—though out of earshot, he had been watching.

"Too cold out there. Your turn, Jeffries."

Sam did not argue. He took up his rifle and stood. He moved away from the firelight but remained in earshot; he would never trust Parker.

Lorena sighed. "Maybe I'm the one who's lost her mind—that is, maybe I'm crazy for thinking anybody could escape the Ramseys."

Parker moved to sit close to her. He warmed his hands and smiled at her, acting smooth, pretending he had never complained about anything. He poured himself some of the steaming coffee.

"Being around you, a man forgets his worries, ma'am. You're a soft-hearted woman. A pleasure to look at."

She did not answer. He leaned back and made himself more comfortable.

"This country isn't fit for man or beast. But a good woman, she makes it all worthwhile."

Parker continued to practice his charm while Sam glared at him from the shadows.

Parker leaned closer to her. "You take me back to places where man is civilized, where women wear white gloves and feathered bonnets."

Lorena smiled and sipped her coffee. Parker was enjoying this moment with her. Sam continued to listen.

Parker waited awhile for effect and then brushed the night with poetry. "'All love is sweet, Given or returned, Common as light is love, And its familiar voice, Wearies not ever.'"

She looked at him with a silent question.

"Shelley," Parker said.

Lorena smiled, impressed.

Sam, annoyed, came closer with a growl. "Sound carries up here. Get some sleep."

Sam walked away with his Winchester.

During the night, they heard the howl of a wolf. The plaintive wail seemed to linger until it faded with no response.

Parker leaned toward Lorena and spoke softly. "That poor, old coyote. I know how he feels."

"Maybe it's a wolf," she whispered.

"He's lonesome. That's all I know."

Lorena shivered, got deeper in her blankets and nestled by her son.

At first light, farther back where the seven Ramsey men had bedded down, they could not see Sam's camp far ahead in the thick woods on the ridge trail. They rolled up their belongings and tightened the cinches on their mounts.

Rank walked over to the right edge of the trail and peered down at the valley floor hundreds of feet below. "Devil of a big drop from here."

"Sure could use some coffee," Rollins said.

"You know we can't make a fire."

"So what? They can't go no faster than us."

"Just get going."

Rums's horse had bloated up when he had tightened the cinch, and his saddle remained loose. He punched it in the side and tried to pull the strap, but the horse jumped back around, kicked and hit another horse, which kicked back. Both horses jumped around at the edge of the cliff.

Rums grabbed his sorrel's bridle as rocks rolled off the cliff behind it. Other men came to rescue their mounts, all moving back from the edge.

Rums wiped the sweat from his face.

Rank spat. "Well, that does it. We got to go real slow up here."

"Won't be safe to keep going," Rums said.

"You want to tell that to Ike? Or Emma?" Rank asked.

⚔

Later that same morning, Sam's party on the ridge rode east with Sam leading the way. Hawkins, Parker, Lorena, and Asa with his pup followed. They continued through the pines along the ridge. Lester followed with the two packhorses.

Now they were riding up through rugged terrain. Patches of snow glistened in the sunlight. The cold dug deep to their bones. The pup huddled on Asa's lap; both were wrapped in a blanket. Lorena also had a blanket around her and up to her face to fight the chill.

Sam reined up, pulled out his spyglass, and peered back through the trees. "Seven riders. Still coming."

Parker smirked. "This is your fault, Jeffries."

Hawkins turned in the saddle and glared at Parker. "You got a fat mouth, sonny.

Ain't nobody got us here but the Ramseys."

Parker snarled. "If you call me sonny one more time, I'll part your hair for good."

Hawkins just snickered.

"We're still ahead of them by a couple of days," Sam said.

Later in the day, as twilight fell, Sam and his party made camp in a thick grove of trees and bushes next to a pool filled by a spring. Boulders hid them from view. Sam dug a pit, surrounded it with rocks, and chanced a fire.

Night fell around them as they enjoyed hot beans and coffee. Soon, Asa and his pup rolled in a blanket near the fire and fell sound asleep. Hawkins and Lester were on guard at either end of the camp and out of earshot. Sam stood nearby and saw Parker near Lorena, who stood wrapped in her blankets.

Parker leaned toward her, speaking softly. "'The day is done, and the darkness, falls from the Wings of Night.'"

"Shelley?"

"Longfellow."

She smiled and shivered as she sat down while Parker rolled in his blankets nearby.

As Parker slept, Lorena glanced over at Sam, who stood at the edge of the firelight, and saw the man's glare. Sam, rifle in hand, walked over to a rock near the water and sat down.

Pale moonlight came through the trees to sparkle in the spring-fed pool. Lorena continued to watch Sam and could not resist. She filled a cup with steaming coffee and stood, keeping her blankets around her as she walked over to him. He shifted his Winchester to his left hand. He reluctantly took the cup and sipped from it.

Lorena smiled. "You don't like poetry."

"Not from Parker."

"He's kind to me."

"So far."

"He could never be like you," she said.

Sam shrugged and turned to look into the black of night.

She sobered. "I only meant he could never be as strong. You're solid rock."

She made Sam nervous. He turned away, pretending to watch the woods.

"But I have you figured out, Mr. Jeffries. You stand guard like an angry grizzly—the more you growl, the more people leave you alone."

He finished his coffee and set the cup down on the rocks. He balanced his Winchester in both hands. He turned and glanced down at her, then looked away. She had a way of getting under his skin, turning him inside out, reminding him of his lonely heart.

Lorena drew her blankets tight. "I'll be the same way if I'm not careful. And I don't want to be a lonely old woman."

She looked up at his strong profile and moved closer.

"After Hoag went bad, I swore I'd never want to be with another man."

Sam turned his back, pretending to be scouting the night.

"But every night, wrapped up in my blankets when it's so cold, and with the Ramseys coming, I wish that I had a man like you to hold me." She touched his arm. He did not move away. "Even for just a minute."

She tugged at his coat sleeve. Very slowly, his mouth tight, he turned to look down at her lovely face in the moonlight. She moved closer, so close that her body brushed his. Sam stared down at her. She moved against him, and her face pressed against his chest. Her hands slid under his arms and held him.

Sam slowly, fearfully, rested his free hand at the small of her back. He held her tight for a long while. The feel of her reminded him of the way it should be with a man and a woman. He yearned to erase the past and hold on to this moment.

She clung to him. At length, she drew back, his arm still about her.

"You don't know how good that feels."

Sam stared down at her. Something warm passed between them. Sam could not stop himself. Sam bent his head. She lifted her face. He kissed her lips. A hesitant, fearful kiss for both of them. Their hearts were singing as they felt the joy of it.

He held her against him again, her face at his chest. She felt alive, the way a woman should. His miserable experience with his late wife came charging back to pain his heart, but it faded as Lorena warmed him to his boots. Finally, he released her and drew back.

She wiped the tears from her face. He turned away, his back to her.

"Thank you, Sam."

He shrugged his shoulders, his heart heavy as the touch of her remained. She walked back to the camp, leaving him alone as he wiped his eyes with the back of his hand.

⚏

At dawn, Sam and his party rode on the high trail in the woods. They found it more narrow with the left wall dropping straight down, but the high terrain was still on their right. From the cover of the trees, as they stood about and rested their horses, Sam looked back through the glass and saw the Ramseys' seven hired men more clearly.

"Ike and his sons ain't with 'em." Sam lowered the spyglass. "But they're gaining on us."

Parker sneered. "You've really messed this up, Jeffries."

Sam turned to his buckskin, mounted, and led the way as the others followed suit and trailed him. They picked their way through the big rocks and trees, which gave them cover.

At a higher point in the woods, Sam led the way through a group of boulders.

They had a view of the trail back along the canyon wall but could not see the Ramsey men. Below, a fearful drop to the creek was on their left and woods, next to a huge rise of boulders, with a cliff wall to their right. As they rested, Hawkins scouted ahead.

Hawkins returned with good news. "Easy way down to the flats, just ahead. And here we got lots of rocks and cover. I could hold off an army from here. Why don't you go on down? I'll stay."

Sam shook his head. "You, Parker, and Lester take Mrs. Ramsey and the boy. We'll meet in Little River."

"They don't need me along," Hawkins said.

"I need you to be sure they make it," Sam told him.

Hawkins looked from Sam to Parker and Lester; after glancing at Lorena and the boy, Hawkins knew Sam had to be right. He finally nodded.

Lorena, upset, turned to Sam. "You can't stay here alone."

Parker had no objection. "He's right, ma'am. If he stays, we can make it."

Lorena, glancing at her son, had to agree but looked worried.

Sam turned to the boy. "Asa, your horse is getting lame. You can ride one of the packhorses."

Lester, getting the message, set about shifting the light load on one pack-horse to the other, leaving one of them ready for Asa's saddle.

Sam dismounted, walked over to the damaged Asa, and lifted him and the dog from the saddle. He set them down and aside. Lester uncinched Asa's saddle, which had stirrups already shortened, and switched the boy's saddle over to the packhorse. Sam lifted Asa up onto the saddle seat, then handed up the pup, which settled on Asa's lap.

Asa smiled down at Sam, warming his heart.

Sam turned to glance up at Lorena. She started to speak but fell silent. Sam swatted her horse's rump with his hand. She started north through the trees, along the trail, with Asa following. Lester, leading the other packhorse, trailed her. Parker brought up the rear.

Sam turned to look up at Hawkins. "Stay with her."

"I know what you're thinking, and I aim to make sure that sleazy gambler keeps his hands off her," Hawkins said. "But I sure wish you let me handle this, right here."

"I've got my Winchester and a pair of Colts. They can't hide on that trail."

Hawkins looked around and made a face. "They could come around through the trees, get up behind you."

"Not that easy."

Hawkins relented, saluted, mounted, and rode after the others.

Sam hobbled his buckskin and Asa's lame horse in the trees, away from the trail and boulders where he would make his stand. He took his canteen, some jerky, and hardtack, then climbed up in the rocks. He settled down with good cover, high above the trail.

⊸≋⊷

While Sam held the ridge trail, Hawkins led his party down an easy but rocky trail to a wide clearing. They reined up where they could see a secluded area in the trees near a creek and pool.

Hawkins turned in the saddle and looked back. "Too close."

Parker, Lorena, Asa, and Lester stayed with him.

Hawkins continued to lead them away from the cliff trail, often remaining in sight of the creek in the woods to their left, until he felt it safe enough. They made camp in a wooded area by a creek. They could look out into open country or back to the ridge trail that rose against the southern sky.

Not far from the creek, Hawkins built a fire in a rock formation that mostly shielded the light. He, Lester, Lorena, Asa, and the grumbling Parker had hot beans and coffee.

Soon, Asa slept in his blankets with his pup in his arms.

Lorena stayed by the fire, a blanket around her, enjoying her coffee.

⊸≋⊷

Hours later, Sam saw the Ramseys' seven hired men coming along the canyon's rim toward him. Up high in the boulders at the edge if the cliff, Sam wiped his brow and checked his Winchester and his revolver. The Ramsey men dismounted and looked for hoofprints on the hard ground. They were unaware that Sam was watching.

Sam, out of sight, grimly assessed each one of the nasty looking men. Dirty, sweaty, rumpled from the long ride, they clearly intended to kill to achieve their mission.

Rank looked around, and spat. Then he pointed up toward where Sam hid, high in the rocks.

"Rollins, go up there and have a look. We'll cover you."

Rollins grimaced. "He could pick me off."

Rank snapped at him. "Go take a look."

"I ain't going alone," Rollins said, so he took one of the men with him.

Rollins and the other man moved up the trail, six-guns in hand as they started to climb the rocks. The other five held back.

Sam's rifle cracked from the rocks high above. Rollins's hat spun sideways, then went flying. He lost color as he stumbled back down from the rocks. Both men ended up in the trees. Their horses jumped around.

"Take cover," Rank yelled to everyone as they led their horses into the trees.

All seven hired guns now hid behind trees and a few rocks. Above and beyond, they could see the rocks where Sam hid with his rifle. The terrain protected him from sight.

Rollins spat. "He's a lousy shot,"

"He's a darn good shot," Rank said. "He's just no bushwhacker, that's all."

"Now what?" Rollins grunted.

"We'll wait till dark," Rank said. "Just stay down."

<hr />

On the flats near the creek, Hawkins, his horse saddled near their camp, had stopped to listen when they heard the echo of Sam's rifle. He came over to Lorena, who looked worried. Asa, sound asleep, had not stirred.

Hawkins spoke to her. "You're safe now. Lester's scouting ahead but he'll be back afore dark. I'm heading on back to Sam."

Hawkins mounted his horse, rifle in hand.

Lorena looked relieved as Hawkins turned and started back. He soon disappeared from sight. Lorena turned to look at Parker, who sipped his coffee.

Lorena gestured. "We'll be all right here. You can go with Mr. Hawkins. Lester will be back soon enough."

Parker smiled. "My duty is with you, ma'am."

He watched her very intently. She looked away. His gaze followed her every move. When she turned, her leg showed above her boot. She pulled her skirts in place.

Parker leaned over and shook the empty coffee pot. "We need more coffee."

Lorena grabbed at the excuse to get away from him. She took up the empty coffee pot. Parker busied himself with his gun belt, checked his revolver, checked his rifle, and did not look at her. Lorena headed for the stream.

When she was out of sight, Parker looked at the sleeping boy and set his rifle aside. He stood up, walked down through the trees to where Lorena knelt to fill the pot from the creek. When she stood up and turned, he was facing her. Startled, she tried to walk around him.

He caught her arm. "Now that we're alone, we have some talking to do."

Lorena stood as tall as she could. "Let me go."

"If you don't want anything to happen to the boy, you'll be nice to me."

"I thought you were a gentleman with all that sweet talk."

"It always works."

She swung the pot and missed as he knocked it to the ground. She fought to free her arm. His grip held strong. He came closer.

"You've never had a real man make mad, passionate love to you. When it's over, you'll follow me like a little kitten."

He tried to twist her arms to throw her to the grass. She fell to one knee as she fought him. She squealed and tried to bite his hand.

"Come on," he said, "you're going to enjoy this."

As he pulled her up against him, she reached for the revolver at his belt. He grabbed her wrist with one hand, slapped her hard across the face with the other. She struggled. He held her up against him.

Her belt purse was between them. It temporarily distracted him. He fought to take it from her.

"Let me have the money."

"And you'd let me go?"

"Sure."

He released her. She freed the purse at her belt and opened it. Then she took out a thin wad of greenbacks. She handed it to him.

He stared at the bills. "Not even a hundred dollars."

"That's all I have."

He looked her over as he shoved the money inside his vest. "You got to have more on you. I'd better have a look."

She backed away, her eyes wide with fear. "I told you, that's all of it."

Lorena tried to move around him. He grabbed her again.

"You said you'd let me go."

"I lied. Just like you did about paying us."

She squealed, fought, kicked, and tried to bite him. He hit her hard on the jaw, knocking her down. He laughed. "You think all I want is the money?"

Stunned, she tried to get up on one knee.

He hovered over her. "I could make more than that with a turn of the cards. No, honey, I'm not out here to get myself killed for a couple hundred. I came along for you. First time saw you on the stage, I knew this is how it would be. But don't you worry—I intend to marry you. But right now I want to break you in. Get a sample."

A shot rang out, whistled by Parker's ear. He spun, his hand on his holster.

Asa stood on the trail and jerked another bullet into the chamber of the Winchester, then aimed. Lorena, moving away on her knees, stared at her son.

Parker sneered. "Put it down, kid."

Asa didn't move. His gaze was fierce.

Lorena got to her feet and backed away. She watched Asa and Parker face off as she trembled from his beating.

Lorena drew a deep breath. "Mr. Parker, drop your gun belt."

Parker sneered, smiled, and slowly unbuckled his belt. As he let it start to drop, he grabbed his weapon and drew. Asa pulled the trigger as Parker's gun cleared leather.

Creased hard at the temple, Parker's head jerked back, then down. He staggered forward a step, crashing into a heap, his face in the grass. His bloodied head rolled to the side. His six-gun slipped from his fingers. He lay still as death with his eyes closed.

Lorena, a hand over her mouth, stared down at Parker, believing him to be dead.

Asa came slowly down the trail and lowered the Winchester. A strange look was on his face and in his eyes; he shook his head as if trying to see more clearly. He laid the rifle on the grass.

Lorena, tears in her eyes, went to her son, bent down, and hugged him. He looked at his mother as if seeing her for the first time.

"We have to go back," Asa said.

Lorena caught her breath because he spoke. She drew back, straightened, and stared at him.

"Asa?"

"We have to go back."

Tears filled her eyes. She bent down to hug him. "I love you, Asa."

"Aw, Ma…"

She drew back, smiled down at him as she wiped at the tears on her face. The pup squeezed in between her and Asa.

"Ma, we got to go."

Lorena went over to Parker, picked up his revolver, and stuck it in her belt under her heavy coat. She hesitated, then bent over, reached inside his vest, and took back her money. She left the rifle where it lay.

Just then, Lester, having ridden back in a hurry after hearing the shots, came down the trail on foot. He stared at the situation.

"He's dead," Lorena said. "We have to go back. Right away."

"Right away," Asa echoed.

Lester, startled, grinned at the boy. They turned their backs on the seemingly dead Parker. Lester hurried with them to the horses.

"Ma'am, it ain't safe back there. I'll go, and you—"

"We're going, all of us, now."

Lester gave in and nodded as they moved over to their horses.

Later that same day as the shadows grew long, Sam was still hiding high in the rocks on the ridge.

The seven hired guns held back in the trees under cover, waiting for dark. Sam hunched down, well entrenched.

Sam, certain he had heard gunfire on the flats, worried but had no recourse.

As night fell, Rank moved around in the trees and gave orders to the others.

"Work your way around them rocks over there. I'll cover you."

No moon had risen. In the cover of darkness, Rollins sneaked over to the first cluster of rocks; the others, farther along, but everyone worked their way through the brush and rocks.

Sam knew what they were doing but could not see them. He settled down between some rocks, his rifle ready.

Rank took a potshot. It slammed off a rock a foot from Sam's head. Sam rose enough to fire back. The bullet whistled past where Rank hid behind a tree.

Sam could not see the others as they got closer and closer.

Chubby Rollins got above Sam's shelter. He saw Sam's hat and the back of Sam's head. Rollins rose up and aimed with his rifle. Sam spun and fired; his bullet slammed into the side of Rollins's head.

Stunned, dying on his feet, Rollins crashed back down through the underbrush.

Rank shouted to the others. "Close in!"

Skinny Rums cowered in the trees, then readied to fire, crawling up above Sam.

Sam spun and fired. Rums was hit and flew backward, crashing into the rocks, and died.

Up jumped Rank's other four men, firing to pin Sam down. Sam crawled aside, rose up, fired, and hit one in the chest, causing him to fall out of sight. The other two, creeping along the rocks, rose and fired. Sam shot one in the neck just as a third popped up for Sam to shoot down.

With his six men dead, Rank started working his way through the trees to get a better shot just as he saw Sam's hat. Rank fired, his bullet creasing Sam's head, knocking him back and out of sight.

Sam, stunned from the bullet crease, lay back.

Rank rose with his rifle and started up the incline. He moved more carefully, making sure to shield himself. He made his way up to where Sam lay wounded.

Sam, half blind from the blow, rubbed his eyes.

Rank reared up into Sam's hiding place. Sam—dazed and bleeding—stared up at the hulk rising into the early light. Sam and Rank fired at the same time, each jerking aside.

Sam's bullet hit Rank on his gun arm, sending his weapon bouncing into the rocks. Rank's bullet creased Sam's left shoulder.

Rank roared and came down on Sam and tried to hit him with a rock. Sam struggled, fighting for his life. They rolled from the rocks. Down through the trees, onto the trail, and right to the rim, hovering over the canyon far below.

"Blast you," Rank snarled. He pounded Sam furiously. Sam, barely able to see, pounded Rank. With a furious effort, Sam freed himself for a second.

Rank lost his footing and grabbed at Sam. Both went over the rim but fell into brush that broke their descent for just a second.

Rank yelped. They bounced off rocks and trees but didn't fall, fighting the long drop below. They hit the side of a slick wall and on a narrow ledge. They rolled, still fighting and grabbing at each other.

Sam got in a hard blow. They broke apart. Rank grabbed at him and missed. Rank staggered backward. Sam, also falling, grabbed at some brush, then a rock. He dangled. His vision was clearing.

Rank, in midair, fell crazily downward. He hit the rocks far below like a sack of wheat. He lay sprawled, broken and dead.

Sam tried hard to get back up. It looked hopeless. The moon disappeared under dark clouds. A sudden rain came pouring down on him, soaking him and making it hard to cling to the rocks.

Wounded and soaked, nearly unconscious, Sam had little hope. Feverish and dazed, he prayed he could last until daylight. "Lord, I know I ain't been right for a long time, but if you can give me a hand, I'll try to mend my ways."

Barely able to stay put in the brush and rocks on the cliff side, Sam felt grateful as the rain suddenly stopped and the moon returned. The Lord had taken a liking to him after all.

He heard Hawkins yell from above.

"Sam, you down there?"

"Yes!"

A rope came dangling down to him.

Hawkins braced the rope, which he had around a solid rock. Sam, his clothes soaked and everything slippery wet, managed to grab the rope. He wrapped it under his arms for safety and worked his way up. Still dazed, wet, and hurt, Sam crawled onto the ridge and rolled over on his back.

Hawkins grinned. "I reckon you're glad to see an old cripple, huh?"

Sam nodded, trying to get his breath. "What took you so long?"

Hawkins helped him stagger to his feet and move away from the rim, over to Hawkins's horse. "Can you see?"

"It's clearing up," Sam said.

Chapter 6

Sam and Hawkins camped at the foot of the ridge, on the creek's side in the woods, until early morning. Near a large pool spread in the trees, Hawkins made camp and built a hot fire.

The Ramsey horses and Asa's lame mount had followed them down and grazed some fifty feet away, off in the clearing. Their own horses were tethered close to camp.

At first light, Sam, head and shoulder bandaged, shivered in his underwear, though he was wrapped in his blankets as he reclined against his saddle near the flames. His outer clothes, still wet, dangled over nearby rocks close to the fire, next to where his gun belt rested on another rock. He rubbed his eyes as Hawkins knelt to feel his forehead.

"You're burning up. You could go into fits."

"Get away from me!" Sam snarled. "And get me my britches."

"They're still wet."

Sam drank a lot of hot coffee. As sunlight hit them, he felt better but still hurt.

A grinning Hawkins brought him a cup of coffee. "You're getting old, sonny."

"I ain't never gonna catch up with you."

"You know, this is a good time to talk about your wife."

Sam gave him a nasty look and shook his head.

Hawkins insisted. "Only way you'll be fit for another woman."

Sam glared at him and shook his head again, then sipped his coffee.

"You ought to get it off your chest. My ma always said that's the only way to get rid of a misery that's eating you up inside—talking about it." Hawkins waited on Sam but got no reaction. "You ever going to get close to Lorena Ramsey, you got to talk it out. Get it said."

Sam glared at him and downed his coffee.

Hawkins persisted. "Your wife, I reckon you loved her. That's the only reason you kept changing how you was living."

Sam leaned back and closed his eyes.

"But she had something wrong with her. It's in a lot of folks. They just get all tangled up in their heads. They can't do nothing right." Hawkins leaned forward. "And you was probably gone a lot, so when some smooth-talking dude came along, she fell for him. She was just weak—that's all."

Sam opened his eyes and swatted at something crawling on him.

Hawkins continued. "Folks was saying they was in a wagon, her and that fellow, and you run 'em off the cliff. And you just left 'em there."

Sam stared at the fire and remained silent.

"And all this time, you been driving yourself into a frenzy on account of the way she was. Trying to get yourself killed." Hawkins paused, then continued. "You been hating yourself for letting her get to you. But she'd have got to any man, the way she was. Ain't your fault. You got to admit you're human just like the rest of us. And let it go."

Hawkins waited but got no response. Sam just continued to stare at the flames.

Hawkins grunted. "Don't you feel better now you talked about it?

"You done all the talking."

"You going back north when this is over?"

"No, I ain't."

"What about your spread?"

"I'll let Tyree get rid of it. And we'll file somewhere else. He doesn't care where we settle. He just wants to retire. Maybe up in Wyoming or Montana."

Hawkins leaned forward and refilled Sam's cup.

"Maybe I'll go with you. We can take Lester along with us. He's real good with horses. And I know how to find the wild ones, any place we settle. If you invite us in."

"Sounds good," Sam said.

"Okay, so we're partners?"

"Only way I can shut you up."

"What about the Ramsey horses?" Hawkins said, making a face. "Maybe we don't want a be caught with 'em. And they'll slow us down."

"Leave 'em. And Asa's horse. They'll find plenty of feed and water."

"Too bad about that big sorrel. I bet it can outrun anything on four legs. But I seen it biting and kicking the others, so I—"

Suddenly, Hawkins got to his feet and reached for his rifle. "Someone's coming."

Within minutes, Lorena and Asa, still carrying his pup, came through the trees. Sunlight bounced on her golden hair.

Behind them, Lester led their three horses, along with Parker's and the packhorse.

Seeing Lorena, Sam frantically pulled his blanket to his chin.

Lorena, hurt, could barely walk. Hawkins hurried to greet her and the boy. He led her to the fireside and wrapped a blanket around her and another around Asa and his pup. He helped her to sit on a rock.

"Mr. Hawkins, I'm so glad to see you," she said, even though she was looking at Sam with concern.

Hawkins poured her coffee. "Sam got all of seven of 'em."

Lorena looked amazed and sipped her hot coffee.

Hawkins sat near her. "But that means Ramsey and his bunch took the army road south. They'll be in New Mexico Territory, way south of the Badlands, looking for us on the road to Texas." He noticed Parker's horse. "So where's Parker?"

Lorena shook her head and sipped more coffee. Asa kept his blanket around him and his pup. Lester didn't answer. Asa had an odd smile on his face, not exactly a happy expression but rather one of relief.

Lester turned to start unsaddling. Hawkins went over to help.

Asa, the pup in his arms and wrapped in his blanket, shuffled over to sit by Sam.

Sam's underwear covered his arms and bandaged shoulder, which protruded from his blanket. Sam nervously tried to keep the blankets tight around him.

Asa came close. "You got no clothes on. Did you take a bath?"

Sam, in his blankets, and Hawkins, turning from the horses, both stared at the boy because he had spoken. They glanced at the smiling Lorena, then back at the boy.

Asa stayed closed to Sam. "Me and my pup. We're kind of dirty too. Just let me get my boots off. Go swimming. Oh boy, looks like fun, huh?" Asa took a deep breath before continuing. "My clothes are real dirty too. Maybe I'll just wash 'em on me, huh? Is that okay, Ma? Can I go in now?"

"No, Asa, it's too cold." Lorena had a tear on her cheek.

Asa and his pup crowded Sam, avoiding his wounds. Sam realized, even though being wrapped and half covered in his blankets, it looked obvious that he wore nothing but his long woolies. With Asa and the pup all over him, the blankets kept pulling away.

Lorena smiled and moved closer to the campfire. She knelt and poured herself more coffee.

Asa inspected Sam's bandaged left shoulder, where the underwear hung torn away. "Your shoulder got hit, huh? What's that scar right next to it? You always get hit in the same place? Better than on your right side, huh? I bet you can hit anything that moves, huh? The sheriff said nobody could kill you—not ever. He said you were tough as nails or something."

Lorena wiped her eyes. "Asa, slow down."

Asa could not slow down. "My dad was a good shot, right Mom? He was real tough like Sam. And he could ride too."

Lorena, stunned by her son's reference to his father, who had been kept only in silent memory, wiped her tears again. Asa, currently the center of attention, kept talking.

Asa and his pup bounced on Sam, whose face turned redder by the minute as he tried to keep under his blanket. The pup grabbed the sleeve of Sam's underwear and kept yanking on it.

Hawkins was grinning. He and Lester came over to them.

Hawkins turned to Lorena. "Where's Parker, ma'am?"

Lorena did not respond.

Asa answered Hawkins. "He was hurting my mother. And then he was gonna shoot me. So I shot him. He didn't think I would do it, but I had to, and now he sure knows it. He won't be hurting her no more. We didn't even take time to bury him on account of Mom being so worried about Mr. Jeffries."

Hawkins shook his head, stunned. "I'll be..."

Sam stared at the boy, who tumbled off him to chase his pup around. Asa looked like a little boy again.

Sam shuffled over to where his clothes and gun belt sat on a rock. He grabbed his clothes. The gun belt fell aside. He tried to keep under the blanket as he grabbed his britches.

"Mrs. Ramsey," Sam said, "please turn your back."

She smiled and did so.

Sam took up his britches, stood, and dropped the blanket. He was so nervous and worried that she'd turn around that he started to put his britches on backward, one of his legs going into the wrong trouser leg. He fumbled and nearly fell and had to start over.

Asa, still playing with his pup, laughed.

"Hey," he said to Sam, "you know what my pup's name is? It's Sam. Ma likes it real good. Sam this, Sam that. Sam, don't do that. Sam, come here. Sam, you bad boy. It's kind of fun."

Just then a cold voice snapped the morning air.

Parker snarled. "Everybody, stay right where you are—don't move!"

The gambler came out of nowhere, bloodied and angry, holding his Winchester. His bandanna was wrapped around his head, and he walked crookedly. He came to a halt, glaring at them all.

Lorena, shaken, still knelt by the fire.

Hawkins, standing with his back to Sam, held his Winchester at his side, pointed down.

Lester stood nearby, unarmed and unable to do anything. They all watched Parker.

Sam still held his britches in front of him, his blanket discarded and left on the ground. He looked over at his gun belt; it rested with his clothes next to Hawkins. He let his britches fall and remained standing with only his long underwear.

Lorena slowly stood. Asa moved in front of her to protect her.

Parker snapped. "I said nobody move." He glared at Hawkins. "Deputy, drop your Winchester—and your gun belt."

Hawkins lowered his Winchester to the ground. He straightened again, slowly unbuckled his gun belt—but he suddenly swung it behind him toward Sam.

Sam caught it and grabbed the revolver, his thumb immediately finding the hammer, and fired through the holster. Parker, firing at the same time, buckled from being hit in the chest. His bullet grazed Sam on the left arm.

Parker gasped, doubled up, and tried to hold up the Winchester, but its growing weight forced it down; it came to rest on his boot. Parker swayed sideways. He dropped to the ground. He rolled over and died.

Lorena, placing her hands over her mouth, stifled a scream.

Asa was excited. "Wowie! Did you see that? Sam was so fast. Was that fast, Ma?"

Lorena knelt to pull her son into her embrace. Hawkins walked over to kneel beside Parker and checked his body. Then Hawkins went over to check Sam's grazed left arm.

Hawkins grinned. "You were pretty fast, Sonny."

"You took a big chance," Sam said.

"Heck no, I figured you was a hand."

Hawkins and Lester dragged Parker away from the camp and out of sight. Then Lester went to calm the horses. Hawkins returned to the others.

Sam stood in his long, wooly underwear, Hawkins's revolver in hand, his left arm bleeding just a little. He lowered the revolver and reached for

Hawkins's gun belt and straightened, setting the gun in the holster and letting it rest on a rock near his own. Sam looked at Lorena. Suddenly, he realized he was standing there in his underwear. Her gaze remained fixed on him.

Horrified, Sam quickly grabbed up a blanket and pulled it up around him. He turned beet red as he went for his britches, which were still damp but necessary to put on.

Worried, she walked toward him. "You're hurt. Let me help."

"Get away!" Sam said. "And turn around."

She turned her back to hide her smile as he dropped the blanket and yanked on his britches. Still in his socks and without a shirt, he pulled the blanket back up around him.

Hawkins walked over to pull back the underwear from Sam's wounded left arm. Sam grimaced at the attention.

"Is it bad?" Lorena asked as she turned to watch.

"Just a crease," Hawkins said.

Sam turned and shuffled into the trees with his clothes and boots in hand, seeming not to trust Lorena to keep her back turned. Asa, still chattering, finally lost his voice and rested with his pup in his lap. The pup chewed on his coat sleeve.

Hawkins went over to help Lester bury the gambler in the far trees and rocks, then walked with Lester back to the horses.

Just then the big sorrel came across the field in the bright sun.

Hawkins warned Lester. "Watch out. That sorrel's been kicking every horse that even looks cross-eyed at him. And he bites."

They both watched as the sorrel stopped some twenty feet away. It tossed its head and pawed at the dirt. Then it started toward Lester and Hawkins.

Hawkins backed away, but Lester stood his ground, blocking its path to the horses behind him.

The sorrel walked right up to Lester and stuck its nose in Lester's middle. Lester slowly stroked its neck. It nuzzled him some more, then sniffed his face. Lester grinned and stroked its jaw.

Hawkins chuckled. "I reckon it just needed a friend."

Lester turned to walk back to where their horses stood. The sorrel followed him. Lester stopped and turned toward camp. The sorrel stayed on his heels. Lester paused just short of the others seated around the campfire, the sorrel nuzzling his shoulder.

⁂

As night fell, Lorena made coffee, then served bacon, from Rank's saddlebags, and beans to Lester, Hawkins, and her son. The pup got some meat, and then she served Sam and herself.

Sam was fully dressed and mostly recovered.

"I didn't figure you could cook," Sam said, tasting her coffee.

She smiled. "I didn't think you were worth it until now."

Hawkins, sipping the coffee, grinned. "Now this is real coffee."

They all paused as the sorrel came over to nuzzle Lester's shoulder.

"Never seen anything like it," Hawkins said. "Like they was brothers. And I bet that long-legged fellah could outrun any horse this side the Mississippi."

Lester lifted a hand to stroke the sorrel's nose.

Asa sat up and started to chatter again; he got smiles from everyone.

⁂

At daybreak, Sam and his party began their trek east through a canyon that opened into the arid badlands with yellow and red bluffs and a crusty floor. Small clay hills, shallow ravines, and nondescript, wind-driven rock formations of reds, grays, oranges, and brown filled the landscape.

Sam reined up on his buckskin to have a view of a dry wash that pointed to a path through red-black mounds. Sandstone shapes rose in weird formations and arches along with rocks balancing on rocks.

"Our canteens are full," Hawkins said, "but it won't be easy. And no feed for the horses. But we can miss some of it by heading south when we get past that red bluff."

Lester, riding the big sorrel with a packhorse trailing, pushed his hat back and stared at the scene. The sorrel remained calm and friendly to Lester.

Lorena and Asa, the pup in his arms, sat on their horses in silence.

The sight seemed to dare them to take a chance. It waited to devour them in its dry, bitter expanse. They had trees now, but farther on lay nothing but wasteland. No vegetation. No water. No life. Not even a sailing buzzard in the sky.

Now, letting their horses breathe, they studied what they faced.

"No use waiting," Hawkins said.

As they rode southeast, they saw sun-bleached bones of unlucky beasts. Petrified tree stumps and limbs with streaked colors appeared on the unstable ground.

Asa started to chatter again, mostly to his pup, but he became so thirsty he stopped.

They rode all day in the hot sun, resting in the evening long enough to eat cold beans and hardtack, then continued riding in the cool of night.

On leaving the badlands the next morning, they took an early stop for a meal and coffee, along with a few hours sleep. Then they crossed grasslands and, at nightfall, came to reach a stand of poplars with dark-green, sharply pointed leaves and a rushing little creek. After resting the horses, they watered them and made camp in the trees, which provided little cover.

"We'll be in Little River by tomorrow night," Hawkins said. "We can get supplies and a wagon. There should be an army camp where we can turn over the payroll. If we're lucky, we'll be ahead of the Ramseys."

"And then?" Lorena asked.

"We head south on the Texas Trail," Hawkins replied.

A bright fire gave them hot food and coffee, but being weary and exhausted, they turned in early. Sam took the first watch, sitting on a rock by the creek.

He stared into the moonlight and across the open grassland. He began to see images of his wife without feeling pain. He saw it as real for just a moment—her yellow hair and pretty face, the goodbye note in their house, and the big vacancy in his heart. Yet it no longer drove him to the same anger.

In fact, glancing over at Lorena's golden hair in the pale light as she slept, he knew his pain had been replaced by the very sight of this woman.

Sam glanced at Asa, asleep with his pup near the fire. He had a burning need for her and her son, but he felt he could never be a part of their lives. No woman could ever be as gorgeous as Lorena, nor could a man's son be more worthy than Asa.

As he stared into the night, Lorena watched him through half-closed lids.

Her first husband had been her true love before Hoag had ruined her life. Never had she thought to feel anything ever again for any man, but watching Sam with secret admiration, she felt her heart beating a little faster. Yet she knew he had been living in a bitter past and might never change.

Chapter 7

North of the trail to Little River, an army camp rested in a clearing in a grove of trees. They were breaking camp in the late afternoon when Sam's party sighted them.

While Lorena and Asa rested with Lester at a busy creek, Sam and Hawkins delivered the payroll, along with whatever identification they had found on the soldiers in camp and on the deserters. The lieutenant expressed gratitude before moving his command north.

By the time Sam and Hawkins returned to where Lorena, Asa, and Lester waited by the creek, twilight had fallen. They made camp and, though tired of beans and out of bacon, ate hungrily. Asa chattered to his dog and anyone who would listen, causing them all to smile.

"Little River's not so big," Hawkins said, "mostly adobe and Mexican, but I recollect they were right friendly. Ain't no law there, not much ever."

"Maybe a bathtub?" Lorena asked.

"Could be4," Hawkins said. "For sure, we can get fresh horses, and I figure we need a wagon to give you and the boy some rest. It's a long way to Texas."

She smiled her thanks and sobered as she watched Sam walk off into the shadows with his rifle.

Little River, a small adobe town with only a few frame buildings, sprawled in the grasslands next to a wide, shallow creek still running with the spring rains. It had a weathered livery barn and a few scrub horses wandering about in the corral.

Three Mexican women stood about the hand-dug well's adobe walls and hanging wooden bucket. Two old Mexicans sat on benches in front of the single store. A few horses and mules lined the rail in front of the cantina.

At twilight, Sam, Hawkins, Lester, Lorena, and Asa, cradling his pup, rode on into town.

"Oh, wow," Asa said. "A real town with people."

Pablo Martinez, an old, short, round man, came out of a doorway. He spotted Hawkins and hurried over as Hawkins dismounted. "Senor Hawkins!"

Hawkins and the old man clasped hands as Sam rode up. "Sam Jeffries, this is my old friend Pablo Martinez."

Pablo nodded and tipped his hat to Lorena.

Hawkins gestured. "We came through the badlands. We're all are tired and hungry."

Pablo signaled to his wife, Maria, an old woman, who came forward with a wrinkled smile. A handsome woman, she wore a white blouse and red skirt.

"My wife will see to the senora and her son."

❈

As night fell, they enjoyed Pablo Martinez's old house, a big and sprawling place with room for all of Sam's party. After supper, the men gathered in the front room near the hearth with coffee and cookies. Asa, already bathed, slept on the rug near the fire while his pup snuggled against him.

Nearby, Lester slept in his blankets on the floor and grinned in his sleep.

Sam and Hawkins lounged in chairs near the hearth as they enjoyed some hot coffee, and they clumsily got to their feet as Lorena and Maria came into the living room. The ladies helped themselves to coffee and cookies at a nearby table. After the women were seated, Sam and Hawkins sat back in their chairs.

Pablo, comfortable in a stuffed chair, turned to Sam. "If these men come, we will say you were not here."

"They could make it bad for you," Hawkins said.

"The army's gone," Sam added, "and we need help riding south. There could be a fight if the Ramseys catch up."

"My sons will go with you," Pablo said. "They will be back tomorrow night."

Hawkins sipped his coffee and glanced at Lorena as she listened. "Sam and me, we got it figured. Soon's we get to a telegraph, I'm gonna send a message to Elk Creek. Tell 'em everyone's dead but me. That'll clear the slate. Mrs. Ramsey won't be looking for you or Sam. And I can writr a friend who'll go see Tyree and tell 'em we're okay."

Sam nodded as he stared into the flames, wondering when this would all end.

Maria fussed at Pablo to help her carry hot water into a back bedroom, where she was preparing a bath for Lorena. When done helping, Pablo returned to the fireside.

Hawkins wiped his mouth and grinned as he continued to talk to Pablo while Lorena listened. "Me and Sam and Lester, we're all gonna be partners and raise horses. Yes, sir. And Tyree's gonna retire and come in with us. We all pitch in, we'll make a go of it."

Lorena looked sad as she refilled their coffee cups.

Sam smiled up at her. "We could use another partner."

Lorena trembled, not ready to face him, and returned the pot to the stove. She hurried into the bedroom with Maria, who had been waiting by the door.

Sam, befuddled, just stared into the fire once more.

"Well, we'd better get some sleep," Hawkins said, "if we're gonna leave at daybreak."

⧈

In the back bedroom, Lorena, her golden hair piled up on her head, bathed in a big, round tub behind a screen. Maria, jolly, fussed in a chest of clothing, then brought out a print dress for Lorena.

"No one comes here anymore," Maria complained. "You're the first woman in two years."

"I'm afraid there may be another woman here soon—a bad woman."

"I know, I listened. But I think by this time, she not so angry anymore."

Maria spread the blue print dress on the nearby bed.

Lorena, modest and glad for the screen, got out of the bath, dried herself, and put on the robe Maria had given her. Letting her flaxen hair down, Lorena came out from behind the screen, tired and longing to just lie down and sleep.

Maria understood and moved the dress to a chair. She pulled back the covers.

Lorena, grateful, lay down and fell sleep before her head hit the pillow.

Maria, knowing Lorena's story, smiled down at her and wiped away a tear.

⊰⊱

In the Little River livery barn before dawn, the Ramseys had settled in for an ambush. They had left their horses hidden behind the barn at the south end, which could not be seen from the town. A back door led to them.

Inside, they found Sam's buckskin among the horses in the stalls. And the sorrel.

"That's Rank's horse," Corley said.

Crenshaw nodded. "They never made it out of them mountains."

Ike gestured. "Crenshaw, you and Corley get up in the loft. Make sure they're inside before you give it to 'em."

Jonas remained standing outside the buckskin's stall.

Emma moved over to where Harley stood by the door to the corrals.

Crenshaw and Corley climbed the ladder to the loft, where stacked hay gave some cover. They waited for first light, but it seemed to take forever.

Ike, in turmoil, wanted Sam Jeffries dead for killing his brother, but he worried about Emma's intentions toward Lorena and the boy. He hoped the long journey had softened her, but she looked as stern as ever.

The first light of dawn drifted into the barn.

Ike looked around, then spat. "It's time. Me and Jonas will be out back in case they run for it." He turned to Emma. "You stay out of sight."

Emma stood firm, a small Smith & Wesson in hand. "Don't worry about me."

"Harley," Ike said, "watch the corrals in case they don't come in here first."

Ike and Jonas slipped out the back door, hidden from town view, where they had hidden their horses. Jonas held back as much as he could. He had no urge to follow in his father's footsteps.

West and north of the barn at Pablo's house, Asa and his pup came into the early morning light, playing and romping around on the porch. Asa chattered to his pup, startling the Ramseys hiding in the barn.

Asa chased his pup around the northern side of the barn, to the corral. They crawled through the fence to get inside and play by the water trough, just north of an open shed inside the corral fence.

Four scrub horses darted over to the other side of the corral.

Ike peered around the south end of the barn and into the corral, waiting. Jonas did not follow; Ike, not surprised, only growled.

In the barn, Corley and Crenshaw remained in the loft. Emma moved outside with Harley and into the corral and quickly into the shed. Asa, still playing with his pup near the water trough, did not see them.

A few minutes later, from the house walked Hawkins, Lester, and Sam toward the barn. Lester carried his rifle. Hawkins and Sam wore their side arms.

Lorena, wearing the borrowed dress, sat on a bench in front of the old house with Maria and Pablo. They could see Asa playing with his pup just inside the northern end of the corral by the water trough. No one knew that Emma and Harley were in the shed inside the fence, between Asa and the barn.

Near the western side of the barn, Sam stopped and looked back toward Lorena, then continued toward the barn. Hawkins and Lester came to a halt.

"Well, you gonna ask her?" Hawkins grunted to Sam.

"Ask her what?"

"To marry you."

"What would a woman like that see in an old grouch like me?"

Hawkins grinned. "A whole lot of ornery. But women like something they can work with."

Sam shrugged. They walked to the west entrance to the barn and slid open the door.

Corley and Crenshaw hunkered down in the loft, ready to fire down.

As Sam, Lester, and Hawkins entered the stable, the sorrel snorted, danced in a stall, and pawed the straw. They took it as a warning.

"Look out," Sam growled, drawing his weapon.

Gunfire broke out from the loft as Sam, Hawkins, and Lester hit the straw and rolled into stalls.

Sam, his six-gun in hand, scooted along on his belly, trying to get a look at the men in the loft, who kept firing and missing—toying with Sam and the others, perhaps.

Sam took his time, waiting in a stall to catch sight of them.

Lester crawled around boards and into a stall next to the nervous sorrel; he put a hand right on a wet horse pile and grimaced. He wiped his hand on the straw. The sorrel calmed at the sight of him.

In the corral, Harley and Emma hid in the open shed, just south of where Asa, having heard the shots in the barn, hid down behind the water trough with his pup.

At the house, Maria and Pablo restrained the frantic Lorena.

Inside the barn, Crenshaw's shot creased Hawkins's left shoulder.

Sam spotted Crenshaw on the loft and fired. With a yelp, Crenshaw rose up and tried to fire back, but Sam fired again. Crenshaw rolled off the loft and crashed into an empty stall.

Corley leaned over and, seeing Lester rise up, fired and hit the man's left leg; Lester spun against the sorrel but remained standing.

Sam rose up and shot Corley, who rolled to the edge and lay dead and half dangling.

Hawkins and Sam, all dirty with manure, got up cautiously.

Lester, bleeding from his thigh, came limping out of the stall with his rifle. Hawkins grabbed hold and helped him over to the western door facing the house. Lester sat down just inside with his rifle. Hawkins took Lester's bandanna and tied Lester's leg above the wound.

Hawkins slipped out the front door and moved around the northern side of the barn.

Inside, Sam moved over toward the east door to the corrals.

Outside, Harley and Emma remained inside the shed for cover.

Asa and his pup hid behind the water trough not far from it. Harley darted out, gun in hand, and grabbed the boy, who fought back. The pup ran around nipping at Harley's boots.

At the house, Maria and Pablo continued to restrain Lorena.

Hawkins signaled Pablo to stay with the women. He hunkered down on the northern side of the barn, moving closer to the corral.

Lorena could see Harley fighting with Asa in the corral. She broke free and ran toward the corral fence.

Sam exited the door to the corral, his six-gun in hand. He stopped cold.

Harley had Asa in his grip, just as Lorena climbed through the fence and attacked him.

Harley dropped Asa and wrapped his free arm around her neck, dragging her against him, his other hand aiming his six-gun at Sam. Asa pounded on Harley to no avail.

Lorena, barely able to breathe, fought to be free. She tried to kick backward at his legs. He just tightened his hold. She gasped and soon fainted, making it hard for him to keep her upright. He dropped her as Asa beat on him. Lorena collapsed on the ground.

Harley grabbed Asa, his arm around the boy's neck. Asa, dangling from his grip, gasped and fought for air, trying to grip and pull Harley's arm away, but failed.

Harley aimed his six-gun at Sam, who held his weapon ready. "Drop it or I'll break his neck," Harley said.

Asa pretended to faint and dragged his own person down until Harley let go. Asa hit the dirt and didn't move.

Harley pointed his gun down at the fallen Lorena and yelled, "Drop it or she's dead!"

Asa rose up and grabbed Harley by the boot, yanking and upending him. Harley fell on his rump as Asa landed on him. Harley beat Asa to near unconscious and got to his feet, gun in hand.

Sam waited for a clear shot, but suddenly Lorena rose up in the line of fire.

Lorena, on her feet, fought to yank Harley's gun from his hand but failed as he knocked her back down. Harley, gun still in hand, turned to Sam.

Again, Harley aimed at Lorena on the ground. "Drop it, Jeffries."

Sam heard Ike behind him. "You heard him."

Sam didn't move, his aim on Harley. "I'll kill him, Ike."

Behind Sam, Ike could fire but knew Harley would be dead.

Jonas stood in the barn door to the corral, too numb to move.

Harley suddenly raised his weapon to fire at Sam, who fired first. Harley, hit in the chest, jerked and spun, then fell against the fence, his cocked weapon sliding toward Lorena.

Numb, Lorena picked up Harley's six-gun as Asa, still on the ground, grabbed his bleeding head. Lorena, standing, started to go to her son but stopped with Emma's cold voice behind her.

From the shed, her pistol pointed at Lorena, Emma snarled with hatred. "You killed my son!"

Emma blocked Sam and Ike's view of Lorena.

Slowly, Lorena turned, still holding the cocked pistol at her side.

Emma looked like the devil herself. Fury had built up within her, hating Lorena for being so gorgeous and for having killed her first-born son.

"You used your wiles to get my son," Emma snapped at Lorena. "Then you murdered him to get his share of the ranch. But you won't get nothing because you'll be dead. And so will your brat."

Emma aimed at Lorena just as Lorena jerked up Harley's gun.

Lorena fired first, hitting Emma dead center in the chest. Emma, stunned, her eyes wide in dismay, fired into the dirt.

Emma gasped, fell on her side near the already dead Harley.

A shattered Lorena turned to kneel by her son and helped him sit up.

Jonas, at the barn door, stared past Ike and Sam at his collapsed mother and Harley. He wiped at his eyes, watching his father take a stance not far from him. Ike stood twenty feet behind Sam, who had his back to Ike.

Ike, watching his beloved Emma dying beyond Sam, swallowed his fury. He had nothing to live for—nothing except to see Sam dead.

Ike growled at Sam. "My gun's in my holster. You do the same."

Sam signaled to Hawkins, who waited at the north side of the barn, to hold off, which Hawkins did but stayed within earshot. Sam turned slowly to see Ike had holstered his six-gun. Sam slowly holstered his own.

Ike stood wrapped in fury at losing Harley and Emma on top of his brother Joe.

Sam waited, ready to draw.

"I'm gonna blow you apart," Ike said. "But afore you die, I got to tell you: my boys, Hoag and Harley, they didn't mean to run your wife off that cliff. They was just scaring 'em—that's all. On account you been riding us. But the fellah she was with went crazy trying to get away, and he drove right off the edge."

Sam drew a deep breath as he grasped the truth. Hawkins, Lorena, and Asa heard it as well. Sam's world spun around him. His mouth went dry; he felt his hand shake by his holster.

Sam's whole life had suddenly come to a stop after hearing the truth.

Ike suddenly drew and fired as Sam, jumping aside, did the same.

Ike, hit in the center of his chest, gasped as he doubled up and fell, rolling on the ground as he died.

Sam felt no satisfaction, no relief. He holstered his weapon and looked toward Jonas, who was no threat. Sam turned around to see Lorena standing near the dead Harley and dying Emma. Lorena still held Harley's pistol.

Asa, blood on his forehead, came to grab his mother's free hand as they stared down at Emma, who was still alive and moaning. Slowly, Lorena's fingers let the six-gun fall to the dirt.

Jonas, weapon still holstered, hurried from the barn, past the fallen Ike and the drained Sam. Kneeling by Emma, Jonas fought back his emotions. He stroked her arm.

Emma stared up at him, her voice fading. "Where's Ike?"

"Pa's dead," Jonas said.

She gazed up at him as she tried to speak, her eyes round. At last she could whisper.

"He's not your father," she breathed.

Startled, Jonas leaned down to her. "But who is?"

Emma, lying near death and barely breathing, gazed up at him. Her lips moved. Nothing came out. Even in her last moments, she saw his anguish. She felt his need.

"Ma?"

She closed her eyes again and whispered. "Cheyenne."

"You mean someone in Cheyenne?"

Emma, slowly dying, could no longer speak. He stroked her face. Her eyelashes fluttered and went still. Tears in his eyes, he touched her wrist and saw that she had only moments left.

Before he could ask more, she died where she lay. Never having felt much love from her or Ike, Jonas felt even emptier and now terribly alone. He got to his feet.

Hawkins came over and put his hand on Jonas's shoulder. Jonas walked away to the corral fence and put his arms on it. He stared into space. Hawkins followed and stood close.

"I'm an old man, son, so you listen to me. Life's been pretty hard on that Lorena lady and her boy, and now you got a chance to set things right."

Jonas choked on his grief, nodding but unable to answer.

Lorena led her son away from the fallen Emma. She paused to look over at Ike, dead like the men in the barn. She felt sad for Jonas, who remained at the corral fence, staring into space. She looked over to where Sam stood over Ike's body.

Lorena led Asa out of the corral and back to the house, where Lester now sat on the porch while Pablo tended to him. Maria took Asa into the house to wash him as Lorena followed her.

Back in the corral, Sam and Hawkins stood looking around at the dead. Jonas still stood at the corral fence, his head on his arm.

Hawkins came back to his side. "Jonas, we'll take care of your ma and the others. You get inside and help Lester with his bad leg. Have some coffee."

Jonas nodded his thanks and turned as Sam came over to them.

"I didn't know about your wife," Jonas said. "I wasn't there."

"I know," Sam said, having already guessed, having seen Jonas stay out of the fight. Jonas walked through the corral gate and toward the house. Pablo, carrying an armful of blankets, passed him and came to join Hawkins and Sam inside the corral.

"We got work to do," Hawkins said.

Pablo draped a blanket over Emma and then Harley. He turned to look toward Ike and the barn where the others had died.

Pablo crossed himself as men from town began to gather.

<hr />

Later that night in Pablo's living room, after supper and with the brief funeral behind them, the survivors had little to say. Hawkins, Sam, and Lester, his leg wrapped and up on another chair, sat near the fire. Jonas, unable to speak but grateful for their company, stood.

Asa, playing with his pup in front of the fire, chattered away and grinned up at Jonas, who managed a smile. Maria came to Jonas with coffee, which he took with a nod.

"Jonas, we're going to Texas," Asa said. "Want to come along?"

Jonas smiled but shrugged. "Later, maybe."

"Mr. Hawkins says it's real big," Asa added. "And Ma says my uncles are even bigger."

Jonas sat down next to Asa and put his hand on the pup, stroking it.

"You gonna get Mr. Spitz back?" Asa asked.

"First thing," Jonas said.

Lorena, fresh and clean, came out of the bedroom and looked from Sam to Lester to Hawkins.

"So," Sam said gently to her, "are you going to be our partner?"

A strange look was on her face. She hesitated. "I forgot to pay you. I..."

Unable to continue, she abruptly turned to the front door and hurried outside into the moonlight, closing the door behind her, leaving them wondering.

Sam frowned. "Now what did I do?"

"You're clumsy as heck," Hawkins said. "Go out there and pop the question."

Asa looked up, a hopeful look in his bright eyes. All eyes were on the nervous Sam.

"There's a priest," Pablo said brightly. "At the mission."

Sam, hesitant, finally stood, turned to the door, and went outside.

With the moonlight on her golden hair, Lorena walked away from the porch.

"Wait," Sam said from behind her.

She stopped but refused to look at him. Her eyes brimmed with tears. Her voice came softly and hesitantly. "Jonas has offered to buy us out, but I want Asa to make that decision when he's of age, so for now, Jonas will start an account for us. Someday, we can pay you and the others."

Sam waited, his heart thumping with what he wanted to propose.

She wiped at her eyes. "You see, I never had the money to pay you. It was the sheriff's idea."

"Sounds like Tyree, all right."

"I agreed for Asa's sake, but it wasn't fair to you."

He stood even closer now. She wiped at her eyes as she continued.

"You don't want a cheat for a partner."

Flustered, Sam fumbled with his words. "I don't want your money. I just, I mean, you could, you see, I was thinking, we could maybe, I mean if you..."

She turned and looked up, her crystal-blue eyes wet with tears. He sensed that she welcomed him to be close to her. He felt as if she would say yes. At the same time, he knew he'd be shattered by rejection. Yet nothing could stop him now.

Sam fought to keep up his courage. "I mean, what if, supposing I, maybe, if you wanted, you and me, and if..."

She waited. He struggled to continue. Nothing came out.

Sam stared down into her beautiful face and forced his words. "So am I going to marry you or not?" He paused, sputtering. "I mean are you going to marry me?"

Lorena stared up at him, then smiled with joy in her face, glittering stars in her eyes, as he continued with a wild heart.

"Assuming your brothers don't run me off."

"My brothers are just like you," she said.

"That's what worries me."

Lorena moved toward him. Sam clumsily slid his arms around her. She felt so good and willing, so warm and fragile, so sweet with the scent of a woman that he found more courage. Lost in her beautiful smile, he forged ahead.

"So how about it?" he asked.

"Yes, Sam."

Sam took a deep breath, barely able to believe his good fortune. He bent down to kiss her passionately. They held each other with warm promise.

"Oh boy!" Asa called from the porch.

They turned to see Asa and Hawkins framed in the doorway by the light from inside.

Sam, his face red, kept his arms around her.

"And I'm the boss," he said, looking down at her.

"Of course," she said with a soft, teasing laugh.

Sam had to grin. He had fallen into something wonderful. He bent his head and kissed her again...and again...as Asa come running over to throw his arms around both of them.

"Oh boy!" Asa said. "Oh boy, oh boy!"

Sam bent to lift the boy up into his arms while the pup nipped at Sam's boots.

⚓

Now as the trail led south into Texas, Sam and his party gazed around at a country as wide as the eye could see. Horizon to horizon, it lay before them like a great ocean of grass, sand, and sage.

Hawkins and a jubilant Asa, his arm bandaged, rode together side by side.

Sam drove a wagon loaded with supplies behind two horses. Lester rode on the supplies and played with the pup.

Three horses, tethered to the wagon, trailed them.

Lorena was quite lovely, wearing a blue print dress, a blue bonnet with frills, and a gold ring on her left ring finger, and she sat at Sam's left side on the wagon seat, her arm through his. They looked deliriously happy as he drove them south.

They came to a wooden sign by the trail.

Hawkins leaned over from the saddle. He read it out loud. "Welcome to Texas."

Asa squealed, "Wowie!" He rode ahead with excitement.

Sam and Lorena looked at each other with love and affection. She rested her head on his shoulder. Both knew well the gift they had been given—a new and wonderful chance at life.

Everything lay ahead, just waiting.

Asa rode back, turned his horse, and shouted his glee. "Wow, look how big it is. And you can't see nothing anywhere. Look, way that way. And way off that way. And the way we come. Jeepers! I bet we can ride all day without seeing anybody, and maybe all day tomorrow, too, huh? And the day after, and even the day after that, and…"

Asa ran out of breath and turned to ride alongside the grinning Hawkins.

Sam and Lorena felt themselves bursting with joy.

The landscape seemed to swallow them until they were but specks moving south.

THE END

ABOUT THE AUTHOR

Western novelist and screenwriter Lee Martin grew up on cattle ranches. Martin began writing in the third grade and sold forty-three short stories, mostly Westerns, before turning to Western novels, of which nineteen have been published. Martin's latest novel, *The Grant Conspiracy: Wake of the Civil War*, also written as a screenplay, was about revenge for 1869's Black Friday and received great reviews by *True West Magazine*.

Martin's screenplay for the movie *Shadow on the Mesa*, starring Kevin Sorbo, was based on one of Martin's novels. The movie was the second-highest rated and second most watched original movie in Hallmark Movie Channel's history. The film also won the prestigious Wrangler Award given by the National Cowboy & Heritage Museum in Oklahoma City for the best original TV Western.

Martin writes full time, concentrating on Western screenplays and novels, often converting one to the other.

CPSIA information can be obtained
at www.ICGtesting.com
Printed in the USA
LVOW05s1612030817
543714LV00012B/1227/P